"The Afghan pig recognized you, and that is why you shot him."

"No! I hate these people. The way he looked at me—"

"Forget your deception, Katrina Mozzhechkov," the Russian general raged, fighting back an urge to blow the traitor apart. "You are an enemy of the state. I know all about you. You were with the man Bolan last night."

"Please, it is all a mistake—"

The general's finger tensed around the trigger as he spoke. "It *would* be a mistake if you do not tell me what you know. I want Bolan."

Suddenly the Soviet officer felt a pistol barrel pressed to his own temple.

"Surprise, comrade," growled a cold voice from hell. "You've got me."

MACK BOLAN
The Executioner

DON PENDLETON's EXECUTIONER
MACK BOLAN
Appointment in Kabul

A GOLD EAGLE BOOK FROM
W✪RLDWIDE

TORONTO · NEW YORK · LONDON · PARIS
AMSTERDAM · STOCKHOLM · HAMBURG
ATHENS · MILAN · TOKYO · SYDNEY

First edition January 1985

ISBN 0-373-61073-4

Special thanks and acknowledgment to
Stephen Mertz for his contributions to this work.

Printed in Canada

When ye encounter the unbelievers, strike off their heads, until ye have made a great slaughter among them. Verily, if God pleased, He could take vengeance upon them without your assistance, but He commandeth you to fight His battles.
—*The Koran, XLVII*

Let no one think that the Afghans are slaves to religion. I have lived with these people. I understand them. I know that more than anything else there's a passionate desire among them to see their homeland free.
—*Mack Bolan*

To the true victims of war—
the children.

1

Incoming!

One moment Mack Bolan was quietly leading a column of gaunt-faced, turbaned men across the folds and creases of rock-strewn, sloping terrain under a star-filled, moonless night sky.

Then came the piercing whistle of a shrieking missile, rocketing in at them from the gloom.

The Executioner and the unit of Afghan freedom fighters responded automatically in the heartbeat before the hit, and in that instant Bolan could discern the first sounds of approaching choppers thundering in from the periphery.

Soviet Mi-24 Hind gunships! They would be armed with missiles and rockets.

The explosion of the impacting missile thunderclapped with deafening intensity, and the force was enough to lift Bolan off his feet, then hurl him to the ground. Abrupt shrieks of the dying punctuated the roar amid the fiery heat of the blast, and flying shrapnel splattered victims. For a moment red droplets rained over everything as the explosion rumbled away. Then the Soviet gunships zoomed in from the northeast.

Bolan landed in a smooth, loose-limbed roll to crouch in the darkness near a granite boulder, tracking his M-16 into firing position.

He heard others scrambling for cover and harsh shouts in Pashto, silenced by the sharper, commanding tones of Alja Malikyar. Bolan knew too little of the language to make out the words.

The surviving Afghan guerrilla fighters bolted in every direction as the Hind choppers sailed in low and fast, machine-gun pods winking, spewing rapid-fire ricochets from rock and geysering the earth.

Bolan heard projectiles pop open living flesh from nearby and saw dead bodies toppling to the ground.

The attack gunships passed overhead, arcing out into the night sky for more strafing runs at the small group of men.

Alja Malikyar's surviving *mujahedeen* sought whatever cover they could amid the crinkled folds of barren rock and sparse wild apricot trees growing nearby.

Automatic rifle fire suddenly opened up on their position from low ground to the left.

More *mujahedeen* crumpled.

Bolan and the guerrilla band returned fire.

The night blazed with staccato hellfire.

Bolan was togged in standard Afghan male attire: *la' jus*, the dark cotton robe of the Muslim hillmen, and turban. His high cheekbones, firm, squarish jaw and stoic, piercing eyes made the Executioner appear at first and even second glance to be one of these tribal freedom fighters. He required no facial makeup for his role as a *mujahedeen*.

Beneath the *la' jus*, within easy access, rode the hip-holstered stainless steel .44 AutoMag, Big Thunder. Bolan also toted a silenced Ingram MAC-10 submachine gun, slung over his left shoulder, while he pumped off fast auto bursts from his M-16 assault rifle at the winking weapons two hundred yards off.

The *mujahedeen* kept up their fierce fire with everything from World War I vintage Lee-Enfield rifles to Chinese Type 56 SMGs and captured Soviet AK-47s.

Bolan heard death grunts from a few more men near him in the darkness. Incoming rounds razored in dangerously close to his position, one projectile whining off into the night, ricocheted from the granite rock.

Then Bolan heard the Hinds returning for another strafing swoop, spewing more machine-gun fire and rockets that gulped up the terrain with ground-shuddering explosions.

Bolan twisted onto his back to fire at the choppers as they thundered by overhead, but in the moment before he could trigger a burst he saw two Afghan fighters stand boldly from their scant cover, each man hurriedly setting up an SA-7 Strella surface-to-air missile launcher.

Machine-gun fire from one Hind gunship spewed twin lines of geysering slugs that took one of the men across his chest, almost splitting the guy in two.

The other fighter triggered his missile launcher. The heat-seeking rocket stabbed through the night sky like a red fingertip, homing in on one of the Soviet aircraft. On contact the Hind disintegrated into flaming pieces of junk that hurtled toward the earth like a storm of meteorites.

Bolan leaped the short distance to the other SA-7 and bellied across the ground between the missile launcher and the dead Afghan who'd been about to fire it. Bolan triggered the launcher before another row of slugs from above could pulverize him.

The second Hind blossomed into fiery destruction and plummeted to the ground in a huge fireball.

Bolan started back toward his position. The *mujahedeen* supplied him covering fire, but incoming rounds from the ambushers who had waited so silently out there in the night continued pouring in too close for comfort. Bolan felt the heat of one bullet sizzle past his left earlobe, then he regained the granite boulder.

He slammed a fresh clip into the M-16, knelt above the boulder and rode the recoil of a three-shot blast at the enemy across the sloping terrain.

Alja Malikyar dashed over to gain cover of the boulder.

Bolan stood, giving the *mujahedeen* leader protective fire.

When the mountain warrior reached the rock, both men crouched for a hurried conference.

The shooting continued from both sides.

"Our thanks to you, *kuvii* Bolan, for bringing down that aircraft," the *mujahedeen* grunted. Alja fed a fresh clip into his AK-47, the Russian counterpart of Bolan's American rifle. "Allah blesses you with *tureh*."

Bolan knew this to be the *mujahedeen*'s code of bravery. A supreme compliment.

"The scouts should have heard them," Bolan grunted, nodding toward the ambushers. "*I* should have heard them."

"You would have heard the Russians. We are being attacked by *badmash*. This valley is their home. They know it well enough to surprise anybody."

"With a little help from their friends," Bolan added, "and I don't just mean those Hinds."

The two men paused to stand and aim their rifles over the boulder to return bursts of automatic fire.

Bolan knew the Soviets had great success in bankrolling gangs of *badmash*, the bandits and drug smugglers along the Afghanistan-Pakistan frontier, who had lately stepped up brutal attacks not only on Afghan guerrillas but also on the Pakistani government and its agents.

Bolan and Alja Malikyar crouched back down behind the rock.

"You mean their aim is too good?" the guerrilla chieftain asked.

Bolan nodded. He had grown to like this feisty team leader during their short time together. Alja was relatively slight of physical stature but a damn tall walker through valleys of death like this one that had erupted around them so suddenly.

"I'd say the Russians have supplied these *badmash* with night vision devices."

Alja's grim expression got new worry lines.

"That is why they have us pinned down so easily. This is very bad. They already kill too many of my men. And Tarik Khan waits for us outside Kabul."

Bolan chuckled grimly.

"You sound more worried about Tarik Khan than about those *badmash*."

"Tarik Khan calls you a combat specialist, *kuvii* Bolan. What shall we do now? Alja will listen."

"Pray to Allah for luck and give me strong cover fire," Bolan growled, "not necessarily in that order."

Bolan tugged off the robe, beneath which he wore his combat blacksuit. The slit pockets of the garment carried all manner of garrotes, small knives and other silent killing devices. Designed to Bolan's specifications, the suit was skintight, with nothing to get snagged or impede movement.

Bolan checked the ride of the AutoMag in its

fast-draw leather low on his right hip. He slung the Ingram MAC-10 back over his shoulder, then applied a black camou cosmetic.

The cosmetic, applied evenly across all of Bolan's exposed flesh, combined with the blacksuit to make the Executioner almost invisible in the darkness even to Alja who had watched the transformation in awe from inches away.

Alja could discern only a vague, inky shadow in the dark and the whites of Bolan's eyes. The mountain warrior chuckled appreciatively when Bolan produced a pair of night vision goggles. When those went over Bolan's eyes, the Executioner became but a specterlike quaver before Alja's eyes. The transformation took less than a minute.

"You are indeed a 'combat specialist,' *kuvii* Bolan."

"And you are, as well, *kuvii* Malikyar." Bolan repaid the compliment as required by Afghan tribal etiquette, stressing the Pashto form of address for friend. He and this tough little hill soldier were more than friends. They had taken enemy fire together. "Tell your men to open up with everything they've got and keep it hot for at least a half minute, then cease firing for another two minutes unless the *badmash* start to advance."

"They will not," Alja assured Bolan. "*Badmash* are treacherous cowards."

"Then get your men ready, Alja. A sixty count from right . . . now."

"Yes, *kuvii* Bolan."

Bolan stood and delivered a blistering barrage from his M-16 at the ambush fire raining in on them. Alja took the opportunity to dash in a zigzag charge toward the nearest outcrop of rock behind which three of his men sought cover, trading shots with the enemy.

Bolan crouched back down to feed a fresh clip into his rifle. Smoke curled from the M-16's snout; the strong scent of cordite burned his nostrils.

He scanned terrain given a surreal glow by his NVD goggles, charting his course in what would be one man's attempt to outflank the gunners who had them pinned down.

His line of attack set in his mind, he leaned around the boulder, pulled off a burst with the M-16 and thought he saw one of the red winks of enemy gunfire cease.

He prepared to move out the instant Alja's men opened fire. His heart hammered against his ribs but his combat consciousness was cool, taut, ready to strike.

Welcome to Afghanistan, where the rape of a nation is resisted today by scattered bands of these brave mountain men who had summoned Bolan to join them.

Bolan ranked this country as priority number one in the Executioner's new solo war against the KGB, the worldwide terror organization of the Soviet Union.

The Executioner had first visited this far-off corner of the planet in the midst of a very personal crisis involving a KGB-sponsored assault on Bolan's base of operations, Stony Man Farm, in the Blue Ridge Mountains near Washington, D.C.

That attack had claimed the life of April Rose, Bolan's woman, and the big soldier still had not worked through the full effects of that loss on his soul.

Bolan's bloody mile of war against the KGB had taken him to Afghanistan and had established a blood debt between Bolan and *malik* Tarik Khan— the same man Bolan and Alja's patrol had an appointment to meet within the next few hours in the foothills outside Kabul, the nation's capital.

Bolan had saved the life of Tarik Khan's son during that first mission to this land and the *malik*, or honored man, considered this a blood debt.

The *mujahedeen* had made contact with Bolan this time by an excessively roundabout method, because Bolan was on the terminate list of the CIA and every other Western power spy agency for his "unsanctioned" activities—no matter how successful—against the KGB.

Initial contact came through a coalition of seven Pakistan-based groups that had waged the guerrilla war against the Soviets since the Russian invasion of Afghanistan: the Islamic Alliance of Afghan Mujahedeen.

Bolan's last stop before infiltrating Afghanistan had been the refugee camp in Peshawar, Pakistan.

The scene of human squalor and misery at the camp had at first made Bolan's gut ache, then knotted it with anger.

Something had to be done to stop the cannibals of the Soviet war machine, damn straight. That is why the Executioner returned to Afghanistan.

They had moved out at dusk toward the narrow passes through snowcapped mountains to the northwest. Hiding from Soviet air and ground patrols, they traveled by night with packs on donkeys.

The only other humans Alja's team and Bolan encountered along their trek were nomads with a camel caravan. The passing groups had allowed each other wide, cautious berth without communicating as they moved across the rugged frontier.

The long march, mostly by foot and occasionally by camel, cut through fiefdoms under the command of a local force, tribal bands led by a chief or a *mullah* of the largest landowner. These, too, Alja skillfully avoided, leading Bolan and the fighting unit deeper into mountainous terrain of rough-cut volcanic walls and steep forested valleys separated by deep ravines and rugged gorges.

The Soviets held the key cities and airfields of the country, but the sprawling expanses of wilderness belonged to anyone after the sun went down.

Alja's *mujahedeen* opened fire precisely on schedule as Bolan had directed, a thunderous cacophony.

The incoming rounds from the *badmash* abruptly ceased as the ambushers sought cover under the brutal *mujahedeen* fusillade.

Bolan took his chance and darted from cover, moving fast, soundless as a specter, outflanking what he estimated to be at least ten bandits, his night vision and M-16 probing the night as he angled in on them undetected.

Closing in for the kill.

Or to be killed.

2

Bolan hurried low along the rocky downslope that would take him behind the *badmash*. He could hear the *mujahedeen* pouring heavy cover fire at the ambushers' position so the gunmen's Soviet-supplied night vision devices did them no good, they were too busy dodging bullets from Alja's men.

Bolan's NVD goggles allowed him to pick his way fast and soundlessly across the uneven ground separating the two forces.

The sound of so many weapons firing simultaneously made only a dull popping in the broad expanse of open country, but the bullets were real enough and some traveled far to whiz near Bolan.

His goggles tabbed them as errant fire from the *mujahedeen*, not always the best of shots.

The *badmash* still had not detected his approach.

He slung the M-16 over his shoulder as he ran and brought the Ingram MAC-10 SMG into ready position. He gained an outcrop of rock that brought him parallel to the curved line of the ridge behind which the ambushers, garbed much like the *mujahedeen* in dark robes and turbans, still crouched for cover from the unusually concentrated fire of Alja Malikyar's force.

Bolan knew the hill bandits had ambushed from lower ground because it provided an easier withdrawal. The terrain on the other side of the trail, on the far side of the *mujahedeen*, angled abruptly into sheer cliff. These *badmash* had not expected much resistance from their victims, not with coordinated backing from those Russian choppers.

The smugglers probably were counting on their night vision goggles to help make quick work of the *mujahedeen*, whereupon the bandits could appropriate all their weapons, munitions and supplies.

Alja had told Bolan that the price of an AK-47 automatic rifle in Miran Shah, on the Pakistan side of the border, was $2,800. In Pakitia, ten AK-47 bullets cost six dollars, though in Kandahar it was said a *badmash* leader claimed to have bought one thousand of the same bullets from Soviet soldiers for a kilo of hashish.

The Kabul Pass, which cuts through the Hindu Kush separating Afghanistan from Pakistan, has been a major drug pipeline for centuries.

Bolan positioned himself at a good vantage spot from which to observe for a moment, but not be caught in the incoming fire from the *mujahedeen*. He decided on a strategy.

The gunfire from Alja's men ceased abruptly, and for a moment silence reigned.

The Executioner leaped from his cover onto a

group of three bandits crouched below the ridge that protected them from the gunfire of the *mujahedeen*. These three were blocked from the view of the other seven *badmash* by an outcrop of rock.

Bolan decided to take out this trio as quietly as possible, giving him a better edge over the seven on the other side of the outcrop.

Some of the *badmash* beyond view opened fire at the *mujahedeen*. The racket of their AKs on full auto helped drown out Bolan's silent attack, and all the while he hoped like hell that Alja Malikyar's men would hold their fire.

These three had their attention focused on stealing cautious glances over the ridge at the higher ground where the *mujahedeen* had dug in and so abruptly stopped shooting.

The darkness of night seemed to shift slightly, nothing more, and Death came at the two closest to Bolan when he plowed into them from above and at an angle. He wrapped an arm around each of them and took the men with him in a tumbling fall that keeled over the third in a startled series of grunts that were lost beneath the gunfire from the remaining *badmash*.

Bolan grabbed the skull of each man he had dragged down, gripping their heads like a pair of stones. Then he cracked them with all his strength.

The two dazed men toppled to either side, their brains leaking from their ears, faces frozen masks of death.

The third bandit reacted as fast as a striking scorpion, his wiry body scrambling on all fours trying to escape Bolan, mouth opening to shout warning to the others that Death had come for them.

Bolan left the two kills and moved faster. He grabbed the guy by the ankle and tugged with enough strength to flip him onto the ground. Then the Executioner pounced, his combat knife slashing before this one's squeal of surprise and fear could reach his lips. Bolan pinned the man, then turned him with one strong movement. Blood spurted across the ground as one back-swipe of the blade brought instant death. . . and bought a few more heartbeats of advantage for the nightstalker named Bolan.

He cleaned blood off the blade on the robe of one of the corpses, then sheathed the blade on the move and shouldered the silenced MAC-10 SMG. He estimated he had another thirty to thirty-five seconds before Alja's men would recommence firing. He started for the dividing rock formation that blocked his attack from view of the other bandits, some of whom continued to pull off single shots across the clearing.

He almost reached the cluster of boulders when battle-honed senses caught movement coming around the far side of the heap of stone. Bolan fell into a low crouch, icy eyes and ready weapon probing the night.

One of the hill bandits coming over with a message from the boss man.

The guy saw Bolan and started to open his mouth to shout, at the same time swinging his AK-47 around at Bolan.

The Executioner triggered a silenced blast from the MAC-10 that widened the guy's mouth into a big black hole that gushed black blood, the killing and the dying both silent enough to be lost beneath the sniping fire of the cannibals on the other side of the rock.

Bolan hurried to the summit of rock and stayed in a low crouch. He opened fire on the six men huddled beneath a continuation of the ridge.

The two nearest Bolan died instantly, plunging face forward into the rock, backs shredded and gushing blood.

The next two down the line began swinging around in Bolan's direction, looking for targets, but their night vision goggles could not discern their attacker.

The second duo at the far end tried falling away from what they knew to be coming, tracking their AKs forward into firing positions, backpedaling to seek cover.

Bolan took out the first pair with quick bursts.

The two had their rifles halfway tracked on target. The impact of the lethal hail lifted them off their feet and slammed them onto their backs and into Hell or Paradise, Bolan did not give a damn.

The last two managed to bring their weapons around to firing position. They fanned apart from each other. The one on the right unleashed a burst.

Bolan had already dived sideways in a combat roll and came up well out of the bandits' line of fire.

The bandits crouched, tense, looking around with night-vision-goggled eyes, the snouts of their rifles panning the gloom. They did not step close enough together, figuring they'd be taken out with a single quick barrage from the MAC-10; to take out one meant Bolan must pinpoint his position to the other.

The Executioner triggered a blast that sent the guy on the right into a wide-armed deadfall to the ground.

The other man saw the winking Ingram and fired, but he missed Bolan because the nightfighter had already gone into another roll. The Executioner came out of the roll with the MAC-10 blazing, his hands shuddering from the motion of the cooking SMG as the deadly stream of silenced sizzlers pulped the last hill bandit.

ALJA MALIKYAR GLANCED NERVOUSLY at the luminous dials of the Russian wristwatch that he'd taken from the body of a Soviet major after the ambush of an armored column six months ago on the "black road," the Kabul-Jalalabad highway.

Six seconds...and Alja intended to order his four surviving men to open fire on the position of the *badmash*, even though the sniping from the hill bandits had ceased at least half a minute ago.

Alja decided to give the American an additional

fifteen seconds. The *mujahedeen* team leader wanted the ''combat specialist'' from across the ocean to have every last edge, but Alja somehow sensed that it was already too late for someone.

Death hung in the air.

Then he heard the American call just loud enough for stony words to carry on the night wind.

''Alja, it's finished down here. I'm coming up. Tell your men.''

Alja translated Bolan's words into Pashto for those of his team who did not speak English. Then he called back to the darkness.

''They will not fire. Come forward, *kuvii* Bolan.''

Alja relaxed. A sense of finality as well as death filled the hellzone. The big American's voice clearly told who had won out there. Alja Malikyar strained his eyes but could neither see nor hear the approaching soldier.

Alja had grown up working the fields with his father and brother in a village near Gardez, the capital of Pakitia province. When the resistance struggle gathered momentum even before the Soviet Union intervened, Alja joined the *mujahedeen* in the mountains. He often worried about his father, too old and obstinate to leave the village, but his mother and brothers had gone to a refugee camp in Bannu in Pakistan.

At that moment, the darkness somehow seemed to shift and the American materialized, sliding up the night vision goggles as he reached the *mujahe-deen*.

"Well done, my friends."

"And you, *kuvii* Bolan. You must truly have some Afghan blood in you."

"We must hurry to make up for lost time, *kuvii* Malikyar. We leave our dead."

Alja nodded.

"And so we shall, for their souls are already in Paradise with Mohammed—martyrs of Islam."

Bolan nodded his understanding of Muslim belief and slipped the NVD goggles back into place, again one with the dark.

"Let's move out."

"As you say."

Alja issued orders to his surviving men and the whittled-down patrol continued on through the night across terrain that became more rugged every step of the way.

Alja Malikyar needed no prompting. *Malik* Tarik Khan had stressed the importance of their rendez-vous in the mountains over Kabul, still a several-hour march away.

Hundreds of thousands of Afghan lives are at stake, *malik* Khan had emphasized to Alja before sending him to meet and return with Bolan. Their fate rides on the shoulders of one man, the one called the Executioner, and he may already be too late.

Alja felt an eerie chill as he jogged alongside this

man in blacksuit whom he could not see and could barely hear.

It was as if the shadow of Allah's angel of Death ran with Alja.

3

"Bolan, my friend, my brother. Welcome."

The two hellgrounders greeted each other in the Afghan manner, the right arm extended to grasp the other's forearm.

"*Malik* Tarik Khan, it is good to see you again. You look well."

The leader of the *mujahedeen* was garbed a bit better than most of his followers. He wore a handsomely embroidered vest, stout riding boots, with two bandoliers crossing his chest and a third wrapped around his waist, exactly as Bolan had last seen him during the Executioner's previous strike into Afghanistan.

The rebel chieftain had dealt the Soviets a number of hard defeats. The area east of Kabul leading to the Khyber Pass to Pakistan had long been one of the rallying points of Afghan resistance.

To the Afghans, Tarik Khan was a symbol of the best they had—conversant in Western ways yet a devout believer in the traditional Afghan values and religion. To the Soviets, the man who now greeted

Bolan was the most dangerous foe they faced, his command formed into tactical units rather than loose bands or groups.

"Times here are very hard," Tarik Khan told Bolan matter-of-factly. "The Russian animals from the north show no indication of withdrawing from our land. Yet there is good news, too. My son and wife are safe in Pakistan, my son fully recovered from his burns, thanks to you and Allah's mercy. Join us now, for you are one of us. See, Alja already informs the others of your deeds of bravery."

"With a bit of embroidery, I'm sure." Bolan grunted a chuckle. "I got here fast as I could, *malik* Khan."

"And there may still be time. Would you care for food?"

The *mujahedeen* camp was too spread out and it was too dark for an accurate head count, but there were at least twenty men.

Alja and his men were already unwinding from the long trek, as the guerrilla leader had pointed out. The *mujahedeen* squatted about, not lighting fires, maintaining a blackout, conversing in low voices in Pashto, sipping *chai* or cold tea, wolfing down dried goat and *nan*, chunks of dry bread.

Bolan had acquired a liking for Afghan food, but at the moment all he could think of was the mission. He felt too keyed for action to have an appetite.

"Thank you but I prefer to discuss the next phase of our operation."

"You feel up to it?" the *malik* asked. "It has been a long journey for you."

"I'm more than ready."

"This way, then."

The *mujahedeen* leader led Bolan away from the others, up a short incline to a promontory that overlooked the Kabul Valley and the capital of this war-ravaged corner of the world.

Kabul.

Exotic as hell but not much from an overlook at night, at a distance of several miles. They might call it a large town back in the States, never a city.

Kabul squatted squarely in a desert basin against one of the most rugged scenic backdrops in the Kush, the contrast of civilization against untamable frontier as harsh as the contrasts of the country itself, a land half desert, half mountain, where the base of the economy, what there was of it, was agricultural with temperatures ranging from 120° in the summer to -20° in the winter.

Still, the Russians wanted Afghanistan.

Another step toward the world domination the cannibals in the Kremlin snickered about, just as Hitler had. And just as in Hitler's time, no one listened.

The Russians wanted Afghanistan, their neighbor to the south.

So Russia took Afghanistan.

And no one seemed to give a damn except for a few people in the States and the fighters of the *mujahedeen:* soldiers of God; holy warriors of Afghanistan.

And a man named Bolan.

Bolan cared plenty.

The Russians were closer to the oil fields now, to the Persian Gulf and the warm-water seaports that Russia had sought for centuries.

The way things were going now, Iran, Pakistan and Iraq were in the same situation as Poland and Czechoslovakia in the final minutes before Hitler went for total control.

That was the scenario being acted out day by day in Libya, Lebanon, Iraq, Iran and, right now, for Mack Bolan in Afghanistan. And if the cannibals in the Kremlin played it right they would succeed in attaining their objective before the end of this century. Then everyone would be subjected to a totalitarian society unless something changed and damn fast.

The Russians had already expanded the airfields at Khandahar and Shindad to accommodate strategic bombers, putting them within easy striking distance of the Persian Gulf and the Straits of Hormuz, through which most of the world's oil must flow.

It had been some journey for Bolan from the States forty-eight hours ago to this promontory overlooking Kabul. But that trip was nothing compared to the hellroad that brought the Executioner to this point in time and space and sudden death from a war in a place called Vietnam where Bolan's odyssey truly began.

Mack Bolan earned the title the Executioner for his many successful sniper missions into the north with his top-notch penetration squad, Able Team. Bolan had simultaneously earned the name Sergeant Mercy for his humane treatment of all Vietnamese civilians he encountered; they were what the war was all about as far as Bolan was concerned

This combination of compassionate human being and jungle-warfare expert *extraordinaire* forged one of the most magnificent human fighting machines ever produced by the United States or any nation.

Bolan's Vietnam soldiering for his government ended abruptly when the young sergeant was granted an emergency leave to bury his family—mother, father and younger sister—victims of Mafia loan-sharking.

After much soul-searching, a highly principled soldier declared an unprecedented, wholly illegal, one-man war against the Mob and actually succeeded during a series of dazzling campaigns in bringing that cancerous growth on society to its knees, where a retoughened legal system could begin dealing with the ones who had somehow escaped the Executioner's sights.

That period of Bolan's life concluded with an off-the-record White House pardon for Bolan if he agreed to channel his superior capabilities toward antiterrorist activities. This had seemed a worthy enough enterprise. Bolan accepted the deal.

During the course of his tenure as head man of America's covert antiterrorist operations, Bolan reached the realization that worldwide terrorism was only a tentacle of an evil even more widespread and world-encompassing than the Mafia ever hoped to be.

The KGB.

Bolan had spent enough time on a mission inside the Soviet Union to know that Russians as a people—the working stiffs on the street, in the homes—were not such a bad lot, but the wrong ones, the bad ones, had grabbed all the power the way they often do in dictatorships and democracies alike.

The KGB was the terror of the evil that spread from the Kremlin.

The impact of the KGB on world terrorism stabbed home to Bolan like a bayonet through the gut when they killed April Rose. He had fingered the mastermind behind that deed and executed him in the Oval Office, in front of the President of the United States.

Once more the Executioner was beyond sanction.

Bolan had come full circle.

The Executioner had commenced his hottest mile yet against an enemy with seven hundred thousand agents worldwide who had Bolan's name and description at the top of their hit lists, and the same went for his own government's espionage agencies.

The Executioner traveled alone again, fighting impossible odds. But for this man, with this life history, there is no other way: no way of dodging a commitment, a duty, and, yeah, think it all the way through, no way to avoid facing the evil product of an evolutionary process that had nurtured the self-destructive strain personified by the likes of Mafia and terrorists and KGB.

It seemed to Bolan that his own life was War Everlasting, and since the death of April he had rarely allowed anything but his devotion to this duty to occupy his every waking hour as a way of dealing with his loss.

Bolan knew that when his violent end came—as he had expected it to every minute of his life since Vietnam—then by God this warrior's life would mean something, for he would have died taking his moment in this continuum and would have bought that evolutionary process maybe just a little more time to find its own way of purging the evil.

A breeze nipping across the observation point made Bolan aware that he and Tarik Khan had been standing together gazing down over the valley and Kabul, not speaking for... Bolan had lost track of the time.

"It is good for a man to contemplate his mortality at a time such as this," Tarik Khan said gravely. "You may meet your death in Kabul this night, my friend. Does this bother you?"

"Who's the man I'm supposed to meet?"

"Very well, we will not speak of it. A CIA man awaits you tonight."

"You know how they feel about me."

"Not this one. His name is Lansdale."

The name clicked. Bolan and an agent of that name had connected in Tripoli during the Executioner's bust-up of a Libya connection when Bolan's work had been government sanctioned.

"I knew a Lansdale from Boston."

"Uh, I believe this gentleman is from your province of Texas. He contacted our people. I have met with him personally. He tells us he is in Kabul to obtain vital intelligence estimates that he has offered to share with us in trade for our help. I trust him, *kuvii* Bolan."

"If it's the same Lansdale, then so do I. He is a good man. Where do I find him?"

The *malik* gave Bolan an address, in the Shar-I-Nau quarter near Bebe Magh Boulevard, that Bolan memorized.

"Do not try to call him. No telephone in Kabul is safe from Russian ears."

"Does he know I'm coming to see him?"

"It was Mr. Lansdale's request that we attempt to bring you here. He is expecting you. He knows how important this mission is."

Important.

An understatement.

The Devil's Rain, the Soviet army called it.

The mainstay of Soviet operations in Afghanistan, Bolan knew, had long been the large-scale sweep: an armored force blitzing or pushing through a geographical barrier, the ground-force operations given support by air strikes using chemical or conventional munitions. The objective: to destroy the agriculture, and force the people to flee the area.

Chemical weapons are indispensable for such purposes. The Soviets fly over an area, drop a few bombs of, say, Yellow Rain, the fatal tricothecene toxin, and after the inhabitants have witnessed friends and family die painful, squealing deaths, they are damn well going to leave before the Soviets come back.

Bolan had heard that the Soviets want Afghanistan; they don't want Afghans.

The atrocities had begun even before the Soviets arrived. The previous Communist-coup regime of Nur Mohammad Taraki was marked by a reign of terror that resulted in his ouster and execution. The Kabul regime has admitted that twelve thousand Afghans were killed by Taraki; the actual total is doubtless much higher. Many of them were the leaders and educated people of Afghanistan, those whose guidance has been sorely missed.

Neither the Soviets nor the Afghan people have given an inch since the Soviet invasion.

More than half a million Afghans have been slaughtered in the years of Soviet occupation. More than three million of a prewar population of sixteen million are refugees in Pakistan and Iran, the largest refugee population anywhere in the world.

The Soviets continue to maintain their strategy of methodically clearing large areas of the countryside of any people, agriculture and infrastructure that can support a guerrilla war.

And now the Soviets had the Devil's Rain.

Western intelligence sources did not have enough information to give it an official tag and knew only what Lansdale had heard and passed on.

A regional KGB gangster, a General Voukelitch, was overseeing the development of a new strain of chemical weapon that supposedly made Yellow Rain a child's toy by comparison.

The formula had been worked into an easily mass-produced horror only in the past month or so, but the first batch was said to be nearly complete in a special laboratory kept top secret in one of the Soviet outposts that dot the Afghan countryside.

The first batch of Devil's Rain was said to be within days of being ready for use, if it wasn't already, and the result under General Voukelitch's direct supervision would be any Afghan's nightmare: the large-scale dousing of the mountains of the Khyber Pass. This access way was the principal escape route for refugees fleeing their devastated homeland carrying with them all manner of intelligence data for Western espionage agencies eager to know details of the war raging in Afghanistan.

If the Afghans left their strategic homeland,

good; if they left dead, all the better, went Soviet thinking.

The Devil's Rain was said to be a colorless, odorless gas that would not only kill its victims on contact but would also contaminate a widespread area even amid atmospheric turbulence like the high altitudes of the pass. The contamination would last for up to a month and would affect anyone not wearing protective garb, which only the Soviets possessed. The objective of General Voukelitch's plan was to slaughter all future refugees fleeing to Pakistan through the Khyber Pass.

Cannibals needed killing in Afghanistan and countless innocent lives needed saving.

If the secret lab making the stuff could be identified and hit, the plan would be stopped.

Voukelitch was said to be sitting on the whole thing, unknown even to his superiors, so that if the project succeeded he could claim full credit, and if it somehow went awry, the general felt confident he could cover up.

America's official position on the war in Afghanistan is that it is an indigenous insurgency with no direct U.S. involvement. But any person on any street around the world knows the CIA has covert operations bankrolling, training and supplying intelligence to rebel forces.

And despite their skills as fighting men and their unquestionable courage against incredible odds, most of the *mujahedeen*—ninety thousand to one hundred twenty-five thousand in the field at any one time—still use bolt-action rifles rather than Kalashnikovs.

Soviet losses, Chinese aid, raids and theft from arms depots provide better weapons to some, but a general disorganization between tribal factions results in lapses in tactics, causing a significant weakness in operational and strategic thinking.

Tarik Khan had been wise enough to recognize that under the circumstances his forces needed the assistance of the very best available military penetration specialist to aid them in stopping Voukelitch.

No way could Bolan turn away from this one. No way.

The Executioner felt honored Tarik Khan had summoned him here via channels Bolan had set up with these people during his previous mission among them.

At this moment in this soldier's life, there was no other place Bolan would rather be.

A cool mountain wind ruffled Bolan's hair and the Executioner turned to the *mujahedeen* leader.

"Lansdale must have some pretty good contacts."

"Very good." Tarik Khan nodded. "Very high in the Soviet command—office help and officers."

"And tonight he's to have the exact location of where the Soviets are making the stuff?"

"If Allah wills it. We cannot afford any more

time if Lansdale's other reports are true. We cannot travel into the city. The Soviets have imposed a strict curfew and those picked up are not heard from again. One of the reasons, *kuvii* Bolan, we require a man of your specialties. When you have learned the location of the laboratory from Lansdale, we march and attack.''

''I must begin now.''

''You will be on your own from here into the city and back. You will need all of your cunning and stealth. The KGB is responsible for security in Afghanistan. They have three hundred agents in the city. There are twelve thousand Soviet troops stationed in and around Kabul.''

''If I'm not back by dawn,'' Bolan told his ally, ''don't wait around for me.''

''If you arrive and we are gone,'' the *mujahedeen* leader said, ''look for us in the village of Charikar, to the north.'' Tarik Khan's expression creased with concern. ''Do you think, *kuvii* Bolan, that the attack on Alja's team by *badmash* and the Soviet helicopters means that they know of our plans? Or your presence here? Or was it what you call a coincidence? If they know about us and you and our plans, you step into a trap the moment you enter Kabul.''

''If it is a trap it hasn't sprung yet,'' Bolan countered. He lowered the night vision goggles over his eyes again and seemed to dematerialize into the gloom before Tarik Khan. ''Either way, I've got to get to Lansdale and find out what he knows.''

"Allah will protect you," the *mujahedeen* leader assured the already fading voice.

No answer.

The Executioner was gone.

Into Kabul.

On foot.

It was time to penetrate the belly of the monster.

Bolan intended this to be a quick intel gathering probe.

But he was ready for anything.

4

The nighthitter in combat black entered the capital of Afghanistan from the north through the suburb of Lashkar to avoid the bridge that crossed the Kabul River. The waterway would have a Soviet or Afghan military checkpoint or both.

The dark streets had the aura of a ghost town except for the motorized Soviet patrols, usually jeep-like vehicles with machine guns mounted on the back, crisscrossing the city like hungry animals of prey.

Bolan penetrated undetected deeper into a once colorful town that had become one huge concentration camp.

At Huzkisar Way, a wide street that runs from one end of Kabul to the other, the nightfighter paused longer than he cared to while a truck, the rear enclosed with barbed wire caging the shadows of four young men, motored by slowly with a spotlight probing shadows.

The men did not see Bolan.

The truck moved on in its forcible "recruiting" of Afghans, many of them fourteen- and fifteen-year-olds, into the militia to be herded off to rudimentary training camps and then to the front. The vehicle disappeared around a far corner.

Bolan continued deeper into the city via dark alleys and the shadows of the sprawling squalor of neighborhoods.

He did not encounter one civilian, yet he dodged half a dozen cruising Soviet or militia patrols.

The Shar-I-Nau quarter was one of wide, unpaved sidewalks and mud houses. Somewhere a dog barked in the night and others took up baying. There came the occasional sound of not-too-distant vehicular traffic, the patrols.

Everything else seemed quiet, most of the civilian populace asleep, the rest hiding behind locked doors and drawn shades praying to Allah, Bolan was sure, that they would not be next to be taken in for "questioning" as enemies of the state.

Life under the Soviet regime, reflected Bolan grimly.

And a prophecy for the rest of the world if the cannibals had their way.

He held to the shadows, since this was Lansdale's turf and he did not want to risk blowing any cover the guy might have worked up.

The Executioner took a full ten minutes to circle Lansdale's building twice at a distance, reconnoitering from a series of vantage points before he decided the CIA man's address was not under surveillance.

The one-story brick building, set back and separated from the road by pine trees, lindens and poplars, would be called a duplex in the States, each residence taking up one half of the house.

The lights of both residences were off.

Lights should have been on in Lansdale's windows if he expected company. Maybe not, but Bolan felt a sensory tremor that made him swing the silenced Ingram MAC-10 to firing position.

He cut over past two houses to the alleyway that ran behind the house where Tarik Khan had told Bolan he would find Lansdale.

Bolan did not care for the idea of taking a Company man on trust, not with that outfit's agents all given orders to Terminate Bolan On Sight; but no, Bolan could not and would not turn back from this mission, and Lansdale was the only card he could play.

He jogged along the alley toward Lansdale's address.

He heard motorized sounds from the road in front of the house and paused against a lean-to structure where a cow stood tied.

The vehicle, which sounded like one of the jeep patrols, drove by.

Bolan waited until the sound died, then continued on. He reached the back of Lansdale's half of the duplex and knelt against the deepest shadows at the base of the wall. He eased along to two windows and paused at each but both had been latched from the inside, shades drawn.

Damn.

He catfooted around the corner of the house to the door at the end.

The next house stood several meters away and appeared to sleep as soundly as the rest of Kabul.

Bolan crouched, eased open a screen door and tried the door handle.

Locked, of course.

A thin narrow strip of metal from one of the pockets of his blacksuit gained him soundless entry after seven seconds' work.

He inched the door closed behind him and paused to slip the wire back where it belonged. He brought the MAC-10 around again as head weapon and remained unmoving, every sense alert, casing the place before he made another move.

He heard someone crying softly, a jagged weeping from somewhere in Lansdale's half of the duplex.

Bolan's night vision goggles told him he stood in the kitchen. He edged around the form of a table and slid through a doorway into the front room, pinpointing the soft crying sounds, woman sounds he made it now, as coming from a doorway midway along the wall to his left. He approached the doorway warily, the Ingram up not so much because he expected a sobbing woman to open fire on him but because she could well be the bait of a trap.

He moved into the room without the woman's

knowing it, and because of the NVD goggles he could see her but she could not see him.

She was in her early to midtwenties, he guessed; pretty enough in an angular East European sort of way.

She sat almost primly on the edge of a bed, feet together on the floor, sobbing softly into a handkerchief.

He could see no one else in there with her; no place for anyone to hide. He could not spy on her privacy any longer. He reached over and flicked on the light switch.

The room filled with soft light from a bedside lamp and an exclamation came from the young woman, startled by the sudden flare of brightness and even more by the awesome, heavily weaponed apparition in black who stood in the bedroom doorway.

"Do you speak English?" he asked her.

She regained her composure fast enough. Her tears gave way to resolute anger.

"Yes, I speak English," she replied in a heavy Russian accent. "What is this? A trick? You have caught me here, is that not enough? Take me away."

"What is your name?"

"I am Katrina Mozzhechkov. I am a Russian national employed as a typist at Soviet headquarters on Fazwah Square. What will you do to me?"

Bolan lowered the Ingram but his finger remained around the trigger.

"I'm a friend, Katrina. Lansdale's friend. What's happened to him?"

"They have him. They...took him from here only minutes ago."

He could see she was fighting to hold back tears, to keep emotions together.

"They? The KGB?"

"Who else?" She looked at him from where she sat on the bed. "Who...are you, if not one of them?"

"Where did they take him? Fazwah Square?"

"No. I heard everything. He had a special cellar hiding place for me with a hidden entrance under this floor in case this should ever happen...when we were together...if they should come for him as they did tonight. I heard them. They have taken him to the military high command headquarters."

"Was it about the Devil's Rain?"

She stared at him.

"The what?"

He read her confusion as genuine.

Lansdale had more than one contact in the Soviet's Kabul regime, Tarik Khan had told Bolan. It stood to reason that Lansdale would have more than one area in which he gathered intelligence and the areas did not necessarily have to overlap. One of his contacts, one of the office staff Tarik Khan had mentioned, happened to be Katrina Mozzhechkov. She and Lansdale had become lovers.

"I've got to leave now," Bolan told her.

"Thanks for your help. I'm going to try and rescue him."

"Do you know the high command headquarters?"

Bolan's intel of the area was complete.

"I know where it is."

"And do you know that more than a thousand Soviet soldiers guard the high command?"

"I know that, too. What I would like to know, Katrina, is why you remain here endangering yourself. The KGB will send agents back to search this place."

A tear pearled in one eye, ready to cascade down the woman's cheek. Katrina Mozzhechkov sat steady and held eye contact with the soldier in the doorway.

"I know when I leave this room, this place of so many good memories, I will never see him again." Her quavering voice matched with the tortured look in her eyes. "They have him. They will not let him go, ever. And so I am with him here one last time even if I am alone, and I linger to savor the bittersweetness of it."

"I can help, Katrina. Come with me and I'll get you to safety away from here. There's hope for Lansdale, too."

"Not if the KGB have him. And I cannot leave Kabul. I cannot run. I have a mother and father and two sisters in the Soviet Union. What would become of them if I defected and went with you? Perhaps my superiors will not learn of my . . . disloyalty, even if what I see in this country every day, the atrocities committed in the name of my homeland, sickens my soul.''

"At least leave here," he urged. "Quickly. If they don't know about you, you're still safe. Do you live near here?''

"Nearby." She stood but did not take her eyes from him. "You are right, of course. I overheard him only this evening on his shortwave radio to his superiors in New Delhi. They ordered him not to cooperate with you. He told them he would disobey those orders. You are the man called the Executioner?''

"I am."

"You will need to kill many tonight, Executioner, if you want to reach him. And you will be killed.''

Bolan switched off the light, plunging the duplex into blackness again but he could still see her, thanks to the goggles.

"It's been tried before, Katrina."

They stepped into the front room. "You'll see your man again.''

She paused when they were at the side door leading out of the house.

"I have lived in Afghanistan too long to believe in miracles, American. And—" her hands rested lightly on her stomach "—I have something of his that must be kept safe. I learned of it only yesterday. I carry his child, you see.''

She moved forward slightly and placed a hand on his arm.

Then Katrina Mozzhechkov slipped by him out of the house without a sound.

He stepped onto the landing to watch her gain the lean-to by the alley. She rounded a corner into the side street that intersected the alley, and other structures blocked her from his infrared vision.

He closed and locked the door behind him as he had found it and faded into the night in the other direction.

He could have stayed to search Lansdale's place but he felt certain the Company man would have kept nothing on paper concerning the Devil's Rain. The top priority now had to be getting Lansdale out and that would take some doing, bet on that. But Bolan had turned incredible odds around in his favor before. In fact, it was his specialty.

During his Mafia campaigns the authorities had dubbed it the Bolan Effect.

Tonight the Soviet military high command in Kabul would get a taste of that Effect firsthand.

And yeah, you could bet on that, too.

5

The sprawling Soviet headquarters, a quarter of a mile square near the center of Kabul, the command post of the 40th Army, the operations base for all troops in Afghanistan, appeared impenetrable.

Surrounding the complex were twenty-foot-high concrete walls topped with curled strands of concertina wire, the top ledge of the walls embedded with razor-sharp shards of glass.

Bolan took a rooftop position on a three-story building higher than the nearby structures, providing him with an unobstructed view of the Soviet fortifications and layout. The main HQ building was easy enough to spot even from a distance.

It could only be the two-story structure with the half-circle drive and the flagpole in front of it, the only building inside those walls with any lights on at this hour.

Bolan also discerned single-level secondary office buildings, prefab, all without lights or signs of activity.

They could have Lansdale inside one of those annex buildings with the windows blacked out, thought

Bolan, but if the KGB had brought Lansdale here, the GRU, intelligence arm of the Soviet military, must be involved. And that meant the HQ building if Bolan was any judge of the Soviet military mind. His missions thus far against the Soviet terrorist machine had indicated that he had a damn good read on his enemy.

Besides the HQ building he could make out barracks and a motor-pool garage.

He did observe some coming and going, though.

A motorcycle dispatch rider approached the front gate built midway into the eastern wall. The messenger stopped outside the iron-grille gate while a sentry came out to glance at orders authorizing the motorcyclist access onto the high-security base.

Satisfied, the sentry handed the orders back to the courier and made a hand signal to two men inside a guardhouse who had kept the motorcycle rider covered with automatic rifles.

The weapons' barrels were poking through special slots in the guardhouse window—bulletproof, thought Bolan—that was built into the wall.

One of the soldiers inside the sentry hut activated a mechanism that made the gate slide into the wall. The rider passed on in, the gate closed and the sentry returned to join his comrades inside the hut. The motorcyclist stopped at the building Bolan had already targeted as HQ, confirming for the nightwatcher where he would find Lansdale.

A few moments later a ZIL limousine, an officer's car, approached the gate and went through the same ritual; the local KGB commander was called in on the arrest of Lansdale.

At each corner of the walled perimeter stood watchtowers, heavy-caliber machine guns snouted from each of the towers, and the men who defended this high-command compound would be *raydoviki*—tough, well-trained Soviet infantrymen.

Bolan saw checkpoints at all roads into the street leading past the main gate. Additional two-man patrols walked beats along the stretches of dark street between the checkpoints and the front entrance.

A penetration by force was out of the question. Even in blacksuit with the night goggles and all his firepower, Bolan could not take on this whole security setup from the outside. He might be able to bust out that way because they would not be expecting that and could therefore be outflanked no matter what the odds, but as for getting inside those walls, the best, the only way would have to be a soft probe.

Bolan heard the heavy rumble of a large vehicle approaching through city streets toward one of the checkpoints. He crouched on an opposite ledge of the flat roof and spotted a two-and-a-half-ton supply carrier coming in from the west. The vehicle was still a block away, rumbling closer by the moment to a spotlit checkpoint two streets from the command compound.

Bolan could discern six *raydoviki* armed with rifles, standing around a GAZ patrol car and a BTR armored vehicle, the 7.62mm SGMB submachine in the BTR aimed at the narrow spot in the concertina wire that stretched from one side of the street to the other, the gap in the wire only wide enough for one vehicle at a time to pass through.

The approaching military carrier shifted into lower gear, its engine sounds distinct on the night air. The truck was a supply carrier of the flatbed variety, the bed empty, perhaps returning late from a delivery to a detachment in the field or to one of the outposts.

Bolan hurried into action, retracing his route via a doorway from the roof to a stairway inside, past closed doors of apartments down to a deserted dirt street.

The building reeked of too many people living too close together.

Or maybe I smell their fear, thought Bolan. Kabul had the same beleaguered air he remembered from Saigon. And Beirut.

He angled away from the building, a crouched shadow and nothing else as he speed-jogged along a course to a point one block short of the checkpoint, then he crossed over.

He stopped.

One of the two-man foot patrols strolled by within ten feet of him without knowing he loomed there, ready to strike.

He chose not to take this pair. He had to make it over to the next street. He let them talk and walk past, two *raydoviki* chatting in Russian.

Bolan knew enough of the Russian language, having studied every spare moment he had between missions. He had already used it with acceptable results.

The conversation between these two, as with most soldiers thrown together during a long night's sentry duty, touched on the subject of women as they receded into the night, away from Bolan's position.

After the sentries had passed far enough away from him on their rounds, Bolan continued on his track toward the street along which the approaching supply truck would come, after it passed the checkpoint.

He heard the vehicle brake for the checkpoint and the voices of the sentries interrogating the driver.

The night is so quiet, even silenced reports from the Ingram would carry, Bolan thought. Until he had Lansdale, the warrior would have to play this one quiet. But hard!

He encountered another two-man patrol walking its beat near the intersection midway between the blocks separating the high command from the checkpoint.

This couple did not know of their encounter with the Executioner until the heartbeat of their death.

He came at them fast, the edge of each stiffened hand slashing downward hard enough to break both necks. The soldiers crumpled to the pavement at Bolan's feet with soft sighs.

One block over, the sentry at the checkpoint waved the supply carrier through. The driver upshifted and Bolan knew he had less than half a minute now or he would miss the chance.

He dragged each dead soldier by one foot until the bodies rested hidden behind stacked hay, well out of sight of anyone passing on the darkened street.

He selected the jacket and headgear of the dead man closest to his size. The uniform was too small, but Bolan thought it would do in the dark for sentries well into their shifts, who would not be as sharp as they should be.

He hurried back to the intersection and stood in the middle of the street as the truck approached, the way a sentry would during a routine double check.

Bolan raised a hand in an authoritative signal to halt, reasoning that since there were guard patrols stationed along these approaches to the compound, it would not be unusual for these patrols to do spot checks along the last stretch to the main gate. Bolan intended to use their tight security measures against them, bending adversity into an ally.

The intersection positioned him exactly midway along the two-block stretch between the checkpoint and front gate. If he worked this right, those at either end of the stretch would interpret the truck's stopping as nothing more than a spot check.

The truck braked, its front end stopping less than a foot from Bolan.

Bolan approached the driver's side of the truck. He saw a second man in the truck cab.

At first the sleepy-eyed driver saw only the Soviet army jacket and headgear where he expected to see a sentry, but when Bolan stepped up, the driver got a better look at the soldier who had stopped them, saw the blackface, the night goggles and started to open his mouth.

The Executioner tugged open the driver's door, reached in and rapidly pulled the driver out, down into a raised knee that smacked the man's face with such force, Bolan heard the neck snap. He caught the falling body in the crook of his left arm. With his right he threw the combat knife across the few feet of space in the cab before the shotgun rider could angle his weapon around. The soldier had no time at all because the blade buried itself to the hilt into his heart, killing him as dead as the driver.

Bolan continued at high speed, staying away from the headlights at all times, everything happening so fast that, yeah, the seemingly distant checkpoint in one direction and the base at the other end of the dark street appeared to be buying this as just another security check by an enthusiastic sentry.

The Executioner dragged both bodies from the truck to an entranceway between two shops that looked deserted. He retrieved his knife, cleaned off the blood on the corpse's uniform and hustled back to the supply carrier.

Bolan climbed into the cab and started the truck moving, closing the cab door as quietly as possible. He pulled out a treated cloth to remove much of the facial blackout goo with hurried swipes.

He drove at a moderate speed and reached into the cab's glove box where he found military orders for the driver's last run, as is customary with motor-pool drivers in armies around the world.

Satisfied, he left the orders where he found them, closed the box and slowed the truck when he reached the closed main gate and guardhouse of the compound.

He stopped the truck and feigned grogginess from lack of sleep.

He saw a sentry approaching.

"Your orders," the guard snapped in Russian to the dim outline behind the steering wheel in the cab at a height that made the shadows only murkier.

Bolan reached over routinely, snapped open the glove box and handed the orders down.

The sentry studied the papers in the light from the guardhouse where the other two soldiers had their machine guns trained on the cab.

The guard looked up from the papers for a closer view into the shadowy cab.

Bolan felt hackles rise on the back of his neck, his finger tight around the trigger of the Ingram MAC-

10 that rested across his lap. He was ready to blow this sentry to bits and drive the truck through that iron gate into the jaws of hell itself if it meant pulling Lansdale out of here and finding out what the guy knew about the Devil's Rain.

The sentry's right hand moved to the trigger of his shoulder-strapped AK-47.

"The orders say there are supposed to be two of you," he snarled at Bolan in Russian. "Where is the other man? Tell me. Immediately!"

6

Colonel Pavl Uttkin, ranking GRU officer attached to the 40th Army in Kabul, resented having to wait for Boris Lyalin, his KGB counterpart, before commencing interrogation of Lansdale, the American agent Uttkin had apprehended less than an hour ago. But the Soviet military intelligence boss had no choice and he knew it.

But now it would begin and Uttkin felt the familiar pleasant warmth of anticipation course through him.

The moment Lyalin had arrived in his chauffeured ZIL, they marched Lansdale down along the basement hallway toward the torture chamber where other work had been going on this night.

They had Lansdale in handcuffs clamped too tight behind his back, each of the CIA man's arms in the viselike grip of a stocky *raydoviki* armed with an AK-47 assault rifle.

Colonel Uttkin hated Afghanistan.

He hated himself.

He knew the Central Committee and the General Staff used him only because he got results even though they loathed him for the methods he used.

His skills had led him to this hellhole of a country that reminded him too much of his childhood home in Bukhara, where the wasteland of desert meets the desolate frontier of the mountains; where he had turned in his parents as enemies of the state when he was thirteen. His parents had killed themselves rather than face slow death in a concentration camp.

Pavl Uttkin had existed ever since hoping he would be the next to die, and until then the only pleasure he could find was in the screams and pain of others.

Uttkin led the way to the door of the "interrogation room."

"Brief me," Lyalin snapped irritably. "Can this not wait until morning?"

"It cannot. Not with...General Voukelitch's orders that all such interrogations be carried out immediately. Voukelitch may be in Parachinar but he has eyes and ears in Kabul."

Lyalin glared at Uttkin, with a nod indicating the handcuffed American.

"You had, uh, best concentrate on the matter at hand, Colonel."

"Do not worry, comrade," Uttkin assured the KGB man as they reached the door to the torture chamber. "Mr. Lansdale shall not repeat what he hears to anyone. Not in this life, I can assure you. He will not leave this room alive."

They stood aside to allow the soldiers to open the door and forcibly push the American in.

A glare illuminated the room with operating-room brilliance. A long wooden table with foot and wrist straps occupied the center of the room directly beneath tube lights, the table unoccupied at the moment but smeared with fresh blood.

A naked male corpse in a corner had obviously been unceremoniously rolled off the table and kicked away. The dead man had no eyes; they were smeared bowls of horror, and the rictus of death indicated he had died screaming. Parts of his body were butchered, his fingers all broken, the ends nothing but gory stumps.

The room stank of a sick sweetness that Uttkin loved.

He forced his eyes away from what remained of the man he had watched tortured, trying to keep his voice steady so as not to betray the excitement he felt.

"What remains of Captain Zhegolov of the security staff. We discovered he has been passing along secret military information, deployment of troops, comings and goings here at the base, that sort of thing. After some, ah, persuading, we learned from Zhegolov the identity of the man to whom he has been passing this information. Mr. Lansdale."

Lyalin glared at the American.

"It would be far better, far easier for you to voluntarily tell us what we want to know. Surely you can appreciate that. Your life could be spared."

Lansdale returned the stare. He said nothing.

"He will not talk without persuasion," Uttkin opined. "I know his kind." To Lansdale's face he sneered, "These Americans think they are very tough but they all scream and tell me what I want to know before they die."

"Begin then," the KGB man ordered.

"Of course."

Uttkin turned to the soldiers holding Lansdale. He snapped his fingers and made a motion toward the blood-smeared table.

The guards understood. They removed Lansdale's handcuffs and roughly strapped him to the table, giving the American no opportunity to resist.

Lansdale felt his clothes stick to his skin with sweat. The table felt clammy beneath him; the light above him was blinding. He wondered if he should bite the cyanide pill he carried inside his mouth.

He could see no other way out and he was damned if he would die screaming the way poor Zhegolov obviously had. Lansdale knew these butchers could make anyone scream with their knives and scalpels and beg for the mercy of death.

Not him.

At least Katrina was safe.

Lansdale made his decision.

The pill.

THE IDLING of the two-and-a-half-ton supply carrier was the only sound in the Kabul night between the gate guard's demand and the Executioner's response.

Bolan made his voice tired.

"The baby-sitter they sent along asked me to drop him off where he lives on the way through town," he answered the sentry in Russian.

"Don't you know that's against regulations?"

"That's what I told him. Look, comrade, he wasn't my responsibility, was he? I'm only the driver and I'm damned tired, I don't mind telling you."

Bolan, the role-camouflage expert, played it with the perfect note and tone.

The sentry saw what Bolan wanted him to think he saw in the less than half-light at the high command's front gate. Bolan kept to the shadows of the truck's cab.

The soldier considered the orders he held a few more seconds, made up his mind and handed the papers back up to the shadowy driver in Soviet jacket and headgear.

"Proceed."

The sentry stepped away from the truck and signaled to the men behind the bulletproof glass of the guard station.

The iron-grille gate slid sideways. The sentry waved the truck through.

Bolan smiled as he put the vehicle into gear and rolled onto the base.

Piece of cake.

Sure.

Getting out would be the difficult part, but the nighthitter had already formulated a strategy for withdrawal, with plenty of room for improvisation. The Executioner's first, his only, priority right now was to find Lansdale, pull him out and find out where these cannibals manufactured the nightmare they called the Devil's Rain.

He steered the truck toward the headquarters building.

The grille gate whirred mechanically shut behind him like the jaws of a trap.

Yeah, exactly like the jaws of a trap.

For an instant Bolan wondered if he had trusted Katrina Mozzhechkov too much.

He braked the truck in front of the headquarters' main entrance, which opened onto a lighted hallway the width of the two-story building. An oblong patch of light fell across the walkway from the doorway. Inside there the Man from Blood knew he would find the orderly room and the answer to where they had taken Lansdale after bringing him here.

The width of the building showed no lighted office windows at this predawn hour. The only light came from the open entranceway.

He doused the truck's headlights but left the supply carrier running, then lowered himself from the cab, the truck blocking him from view of the building.

He saw a two-man roving sentry patrol walk in the opposite direction, paying little attention to a military vehicle that had cleared two checkpoints.

Bolan waited an additional second after the guards disappeared from sight around one of the barracks buildings, gave a quick look around to make sure no one could see him, then tugged off the cap and Soviet uniform jacket. He double-timed it around the front of the truck and up the short walkway, in through the front door of Soviet headquarters.

He stepped briskly to the first office doorway, which was open, light streaming out, to his right.

Orderly room.

Bolan nodded when he saw the four Soviet soldiers. They were relaxing as if they didn't have a thing to worry about because they sat under the tightest security lid in Kabul; three *raydoviki*, bearlike in Russian army uniforms, rifles close at hand, lounged in chairs, waiting for the end of their shift. A younger enlisted man, the orderly, behind a desk to answer incoming calls, at the moment was leafing through an American sex magazine.

The four soldiers reacted a heartbeat too late at the sight of the big dude.

The kid behind the desk stood, mouth agape as he reached for a holstered pistol.

The *raydoviki* recovered enough from their lethargy and grabbed for weapons.

Bolan swung the Ingram MAC-10 at hip level and

squeezed the trigger, the submachine gun recoiling in his fists, the silenced tube spitting flashes of orange-red flame and 9mm manglers to terminate the three infantrymen.

Two of the Soviets caught the Ingram's stitching fire after they grabbed their AKs but before they could pull the rifles around on the blacksuited penetrator. Bolan executed these cannibals, both men spinning away under the impact of so many slugs and such sudden death, sprawling across furniture in a tangle against the wall.

The third infantryman's weapon was rising, but only reached halfway up toward Bolan when another 9mm burst raked this one even though he tried to steer away at the last second. The blistering slugs riddled his chest at a different angle.

Only heartbeats had passed since Bolan wasted the trio, but the orderly behind the desk managed to unbutton the flap of his belt holster and clear leather, a pistol tracking toward the Executioner.

Bolan dropped on the punk like a house, pinning this cannibal backward across the desk, swatting the Ingram at the kid's gun wrist. The big warrior heard a snap and the pistol and skin mag skidded off the desk to the floor.

Bolan applied pressure, pinning the orderly to the desk top. The Executioner pressed the silencer-muzzled snout of the MAC-10 against the punk's chest.

"The prisoner they just brought in," he growled

in icy Russian. "The American. Lansdale. Where is he?"

Beads of sweat popped across the soldier's face.

"D-downstairs. Third room on the left! Don't—"

"You should've stayed home, kid."

Bolan triggered a burst from the Ingram. The soldier bucked, his feet off the ground, then collapsed to the floor when Bolan released the dead throat. The would-be cannibal's tunic smoldered from the contact shot.

Bolan exited the orderly room thirty seconds after he went in.

He started toward the stairway leading to the basement level when combat senses alerted him in time to eyeball a two-man guard unit strolling in through the building's entrance on its appointed rounds, or to gab with their comrades in the orderly room. They found their Executioner, who triggered a silenced burst, and the sentries tumbled backward out of the doorway across the walk, life oozing from them, and Bolan knew he had whittled down his time.

He took the stairway to the basement level four steps at a time. He slapped another clip into the Ingram.

The Bolan Effect, yeah.

Hitting hard.

7

Lansdale's tongue made contact with the pill wedged against the roof of his mouth.

He loosened it from where it had been specially sealed back in the States. He closed his eyes against the piercing light and what he had got himself into. What a cruddy way to die, he thought.

Colonel Uttkin's face loomed above him, blocking the light.

"Perhaps you think you can, how do you say, ah, yes, hold out on us, Mr. Lansdale," the GRU pig purred silkily with a smile that wasn't quite sane. "I can assure you that the longer you force us to continue with this unpleasantness, the more you endanger others. Such as Katrina Mozzhechkov."

Lansdale stopped working the suicide pill loose and tried like hell to register no reaction at all, but he could see the GRU sadist pick up on the tightening he felt.

Uttkin cackled.

"I see the lady's name draws a response. It seems Miss Mozzhechkov was Captain Zhegolov's typist, as you must surely know, and it also seems the unfortunate woman needed a friend. The dear captain told us what he suspected between you and her, before he died. It was that or losing a, er, principal part of himself. The same thing awaits you, Mr. Lansdale, unless of course you wish to spare yourself. A quick death, so merciful. . . ."

The KGB man, Lyalin, snorted.

"You enjoy this too much. Have your men get on with this foul business. We must learn what he knows and what he has already passed to his people."

Uttkin stepped back from leaning across the table, his face flushed, florid.

"But of course, comrade. I only wanted our silent friend here to realize that if he talks, Miss Mozzhechkov will be spared any of this. We do not have her yet but we shall by morning." Uttkin licked fleshy lips. He addressed Lansdale. "Now then, will you cooperate?"

At least they don't have her, Lansdale thought. If he could only find some way to warn her. Katrina would arrive at her job tomorrow not knowing they were on to her.

Again Lyalin snorted.

"The prisoner seems unimpressed with your threats, Colonel."

Uttkin bristled.

"Very well. He has willed this upon himself." The sadist turned to the two soldiers. "Strip him. Then use your knives. Begin."

The door to the torture chamber exploded inward with shattering force under a powerful kick.

A human grim reaper stalked into that room spewing death from a blazing Ingram MAC-10 that riddled one of the *raydoviki* with a tight stitch, pulping the guy's heart. His chewed-up body made a splattered mess across the wall, where he stuck for a moment as if pinned, already dead, then his remains slid to the floor.

Lansdale craned his head around on the table.

He recognized Bolan instantly.

He spit out the suicide pill.

The three other Russians in the room fell away from the table. Lansdale started trying to free his wrists and ankles from the leather bindings but found himself immobile, helpless to do anything but watch his own fate unfold.

Uttkin reared away from Lansdale's right side, clawing for his side arm.

Boris Lyalin was trying desperately to maneuver away from the tracking Ingram to the other side of Lansdale, at the same time unleathering a Walther PPK.

The uniformed soldier reacted quickest because he had only to swing his shoulder-strapped AK toward the human fire storm in black whose Ingram kept spitting flame, stitching this soldier.

Lyalin had his Walther PPK out, tracking a bead on the Executioner.

Uttkin, responses dulled by the anticipation of

torture, barely had his pistol cleared from his belt holster.

Bolan bent his knees and moved sideways at the same instant Lyalin triggered a round that slammed into the door frame where Bolan had been a moment before. The Executioner triggered another silenced blast and the KGB officer hurtled backward into hell.

Uttkin, eyes still glazed, tugged his pistol up.

Lansdale sensed the Executioner whirling to respond, but the shackled CIA man could not stay uninvolved a moment longer. He gave the table beneath him a powerful heave to the right, riding the leverage with all his weight, and the table toppled over sideways into Uttkin, knocking the GRU man down with it. The Russian colonel's pistol flew out of his fingers to land a few feet from the naked corpse of the man Uttkin had tortured.

Uttkin cursed in Russian and pushed off the weight of the man-laden table, got free and tried to get to his pistol but only made it halfway before Bolan opened fire. The GRU officer skidded onto his face as if tripped, the back of his head blown in by the burst from the Ingram.

The Executioner crossed rapidly to crouch beside the overturned table. He untied the straps that bound Lansdale to the rack.

"Thanks, buddy," Bolan grunted as he released the last clasp.

Lansdale scrambled to his feet, rubbing his wrists.

"No, my thanks to *you*, big dude. Sounds like we've got company."

The doorway filled with three *raydoviki* tumbling into the room in response to Boris Lyalin's pistol shot.

Bolan swung the Ingram to take them out, but Lansdale had maneuvered himself into the line of fire so Bolan stepped aside while the Company man erupted into a series of rapid-fire martial arts punches and kicks, taking out two of the soldiers, breaking necks with a couple of stiff-handed blows.

The CIA agent spun with a leg stiffened out in a backward blow, the heel caving in the other soldier's forehead, adding another dead man to the "interrogation room."

Bolan tossed his M-16 across the short distance to Lansdale.

"Here, this'll be easier."

Lansdale caught the rifle.

"Maybe, but not half as much fun. You got any particular plan in mind, pard?"

Bolan hustled them out of the doorway.

"A truck upstairs."

They hit the basement hallway and the bottom of the stairway leading up, and they ran into four more Soviet regulars racing toward them.

The Executioner took out the two on the right, the Ingram stuttering its silenced dirge, killing men who tumbled to the corridor, posed in death like some weird sculpture.

Lansdale tugged off a burst from the M-16 and a soldier on the left caught the hail of hammering projectiles that twisted and staggered him, life forces bursting red everywhere until the dancing dead tripped and toppled down the steps.

The MAC-10 in Bolan's hands issued an angry message of death that pulverized the last trooper, the leaden stream chopping off limbs making bloody modern art designs across bullet-riddled walls.

Bolan and Lansdale rushed up the stairs to the ground-floor level.

"Things never got this noisy back in the panhandle," Lansdale grunted as they made the top.

Bolan frowned. This was the same guy he had worked with in Libya, no doubt of it.

"Last time we met you had a Boston accent."

"So I get around," the Texan replied in a good-natured drawl. "A guy's got to have some fun in life."

They left the stairs and raced toward the main entrance, heading for the supply carrier Bolan had left idling.

A Klaxon raped the silent night, alerting soldiers all around the HQ building.

Two heads poked out of an office doorway halfway down the hall, soldiers scoping the action.

Bolan blew their heads off before they got any ideas.

The Executioner and his CIA sidekick dashed

from the building, Bolan to the driver's side of the truck, Lansdale tugging off a stutter from the M-16 that sent three sleepy-eyed troopers back to eternal slumber in the doorway of the nearest barracks. Then Lansdale hopped up into the cab and kept low as more soldiers, responding to the ruckus, poured out of the barracks, their attention on the HQ building and the commotion around the supply carrier.

Bolan popped the clutch, upshifting them the hell away from there.

Automatic fire from AK-47s and a heavier machine gun opened up on the moving truck but most of those slugs whistled wildly into the night, the rest whizzing through the cab but finding no targets.

Bolan wheeled the vehicle into a tight turn toward the main gate.

Lansdale saw men racing for vehicles parked by the motor-pool garage. As Bolan steered the truck, continuing to accelerate the closer he got to the closed main gate, Lansdale leaned out his side of the truck cab and rode out a heavy burst from his M-16 that cut down half a dozen men around those vehicles like a scythe cutting wheat, but he knew others would take their place in no time.

The truck ate up the distance to the closed iron gate and the guardhouse. More gunfire stitched the supply carrier but missed the cab.

A guard stepped out of the gate house, raised his AK-47 and squeezed off one round that spiderwebbed the windshield between the men in the cab, but hit neither.

The other two front-gate sentries remained inside their guardhouse, snouts of their machine guns swiveling toward the approaching truck from the turrets built into the bulletproof glass.

The brave fool in Bolan's path almost had time to trigger another shot, but the truck jolted under an impact that sounded like a bug crushed under a heavy foot.

For a few seconds the Russian soldier rode like a mascot with arms outflung across the grillwork of the truck, dead eyes glaring at the man from death behind the steering wheel. Then the nose of the truck plowed on through the iron gate with enough force to rip the gate from its moorings, the upright iron rods making ground meat out of the soldier's body.

Bolan gunned the truck away from there under a hail of fire from the guardhouse. He yanked the steering wheel to the left and took the turn onto the street that ran along the walled compound toward the nearest checkpoint; the men stationed there would have less time to respond.

The deuce-and-a-half left behind plenty of activity, Soviet officers snapping their well-trained troops into response, engines of vehicles throating to life, loading up with troops to give chase.

The sentries inside the gate house swung their weapons around as far as the bulletproof window turrets would allow, but could no longer track on the fleeing vehicle. One of the guards stepped outside for a parting shot but he got a farewell death-burst from Lansdale.

The CIA agent plugged a fresh clip into the M-16 as the Executioner powered the two-and-a-half-ton metal monster faster toward the checkpoint. Lansdale leaned out from his side of the truck's cab. The night wind on his face felt good after the fetid stench of Colonel Uttkin's torture chamber.

The Texan hammered off more M-16 fire, this time at the group of *raydoviki* at the checkpoint, cutting down two while another scrambled for cover.

Bolan unleathered Big Thunder and straight-arm aimed a head shot that roared in the night, decapitating the communications man by the patrol car. Bolan steered the speeding supply rig on through the checkpoint.

Two soldiers opened fire as the deuce-and-a-half clattered by like an express train, but too much was happening at once for their aim to be any good; none of their buzzing bullets found meat in the cab of the racing military vehicle.

Bolan's .44 cannon dropped another *raydoviki* as the guy tried to swing around a machine gun mounted at the back of one of the vehicles, then Bolan concentrated on steering the rocketing truck, clearing the checkpoint and roaring on into the night.

Three checkpoint soldiers remained alive long enough to trigger some more ill-aimed rounds at the truck before Lansdale fired a goodbye chorus from the M-16, leaning out backward from the passenger side of the cab now.

The three soldiers caught the withering hail of 5.56mm hornets and died, spasming in death dances before they toppled.

In the truck's rearview mirror Bolan caught sight of a dozen or more vehicles giving hell-for-leather chase after the supply carrier.

Soviet pursuers poured from the main gate a quarter mile back, many of the vehicles smaller, faster than the military transport vehicle.

The Kabul night rumbled with motorized fury.

Bolan kept the carrier's pedal to the metal, giving the deuce-and-a-half everything she had but knowing it would not be enough to outdistance those snapping hounds of hell closing in too damn fast.

8

Bolan played out his only option. He downshifted, pumping the brake at the same time. When he had the decreased speed he wanted, still moving fast, he wheeled the supply carrier into a bone-rattling sideways skid, gripping the steering wheel to hold himself steady. Lansdale held onto the frame of the truck's cab for dear life.

The truck slewed to a shuddering halt across the narrow street, where it would effectively block the pursuers at least long enough to give Bolan and Lansdale a good start on foot.

Bolan ejected himself from the cab while the vehicle was still sliding, landing in a combat crouch to fan the escape route with Big Thunder. Wary combat senses were on alert, probing the night.

The dark street appeared deserted. For now.

Lansdale trotted up.

"Good play, big guy. If it works."

Bolan took off in a rapid, surefooted trot along the road, away from the truck and the rapidly approaching clamor of Soviet pursuers.

Lansdale kept pace.

"You're good at ad-libbing a script," Bolan told the guy.

The Texan chuckled as they covered distance.

"You oughta hear my one-liners. What have you got in mind now? There's a woman, Katrina. . .a friend."

"I met her. She's the one who told me where to find you."

"She's a good woman, Bolan. You must know that if you met her. The KGB and the GRU. . .they found out about her association with me. Damn, I shouldn't have messed with her."

They had gone several hundred yards when they heard the Russian chase vehicles screech to a halt. Shouts in Russian reached Bolan and Lansdale at the far end of the block where a side street intersected.

The Executioner and the CIA man dodged around that corner with microseconds to spare before a volley of automatic gunfire blistered the night.

"We can reach Katrina in time to warn her before we leave Kabul," Bolan assured the guy. "Does she have transportation?"

Their jogging picked up. Lansdale kept the pace set by Bolan.

"She does," Lansdale acknowledged. "The tough part's gonna be shaking those yahoos back there. That truck won't stop those cowboys but a minute or two. What do you reckon, pard?"

"I reckon you were easier to take when you were from Boston," Bolan said. Then he froze in his tracks and held up his hand. "Hold it!"

Lansdale stopped and tossed a nod in the direction of engines accelerating in the near distance.

"I hope you've got a miracle handy in your back pocket, big guy," he said.

Bolan tracked his Ingram on shadows up ahead where his NVD had outlined a parked automobile, a battered Czech Tatra, a stubby four-cylinder job not unlike the old VW bug.

The Tatra's engine started; its headlights blazed to life.

Lansdale shouted in surprise.

"That's Katrina's car!"

Then Bolan saw the woman herself move hurriedly from her side of the vehicle. She waved them toward her.

"Let's go," Bolan growled to Lansdale, not lowering his guard or the AutoMag. "Be careful."

They advanced.

The cacophony of approaching vehicles from the street a block away told Bolan the Russian troops had negotiated the barrier of the supply carrier and were racing to close the gap.

"We don't have to be careful with Katrina," Lansdale whispered to Bolan as they approached the woman who held open the passenger door. "Katrina's all right. You've got to trust some people."

"Be careful," Bolan repeated low enough for the Russian woman not to hear.

He and Lansdale reached the car.

"Bolan, you take the wheel, okay?" Lansdale called. He moved to the passenger side where Katrina waited. "If you drive like you shoot, we're already home."

"With pleasure," Bolan grunted.

He angled in behind the steering wheel of the Tatra, popping the clutch to get them out of there while Katrina and Lansdale bustled to climb in the passenger side.

At the corner of the cross street, the first of the Russian pursuit vehicles screamed into the intersection, a BTR-40 armored job, its turret machine gunner blazing wide open in a full arc that riddled the night.

Projectiles zinged and clipped around the Tatra.

Then Bolan heard the ugly sound of a 7.62mm slug impacting with living flesh.

He swung his head sideways as Lansdale gurgled out a sharp cry of pain and surprise and tumbled against the car, bracing himself against the roof, while Katrina Mozzhechkov reacted with no wasted movement to reach in and position Lansdale into the back seat. Lansdale continued to make gurgling, pain-racked sounds as he collapsed into the Tatra.

The machine gunner aboard the armored car at the intersection tracked his line of fire back toward the Tatra, the heavy hammering of his weapon piercing the night. More Soviet troops rounded the corner and commenced rushing after the little bucket of bolts that had already goosed forward like a bat out of hell. Lansdale was bleeding over everything; the guy could only have seconds left, Bolan realized when he saw the wound; the slug had caught Lansdale in the back and cored right on through.

Lansdale was hemorrhaging badly from the nose and mouth.

Katrina had tumbled into the car from the momentum of their takeoff with a practiced grip on the M-16. She unleashed a burst at the pursuers, but before she or Bolan could see if it did any good, Bolan executed a two-wheeled turn out of that street in the direction they had come, one block over.

He palmed the wheel again, playing the gears, the Tatra fishtailing madly, tires shrieking across pavement to almost drown out the tumult of Soviets continuing to close in much too damn fast. He angled out of the turn along a passageway between private residences, a walkway not meant for vehicles. He knew the pursuing military vehicles would not fit through.

The little car whizzed between a row of darkened houses, across a courtyard deserted at this hour, and shot into the next parallel street over. Bolan veered into the street without slowing, then accelerated more in another shift of direction—right into the path of an eight-wheeled BTR-6 armored personnel carrier.

The troop transport vehicle was lumbering along, prepared to intercept at the next street if Bolan had kept to the roadway.

The driver of the personnel carrier had not expected the quarry to come rocketing past him at this point. His reflexes came a heartbeat too slow and the personnel carrier lurched to the curb, jarring the *raydoviki* being carried, hindering their reaction at the sight of the speeding automobile.

Bolan coaxed a round from Big Thunder out the Tatra's window and saw the head of the personnel carrier's driver explode as the car streaked by.

Katrina hammered off a burst from the passenger seat beside Bolan, keeping heads of Soviet troopers down behind the armor of the personnel carrier. She rode the recoil of the M-16 until the magazine ran dry and by that time they had passed the personnel carrier.

The small car squealed into another almost ninety-degree turn as Bolan angled ever steadily away from the ruckus that already spread outward from the Soviet HQ base.

He piloted the car along somewhat the same route of his penetration into the nighttime city. After they crossed Huzkisar Way he risked a look back at Lansdale, already knowing what he would find.

From the sound of the impacting bullet and the silence from the back seat since Katrina had piled Lansdale into the car, Bolan knew the brave CIA agent was dead.

Katrina turned around, too. She reached around to touch her lifeless lover in the back seat but she shed no tears.

"They will pay," she said quietly, not to Bolan, as if voicing a thought to the universe.

Bolan recognized the three words with a clarity that made his knuckles tighten around the steering wheel. He had spoken those same words moments after April Rose had died in his arms; the declaration of his one-man outlaw war against the KGB.

"I know how you feel, Katrina," he told the woman. "I feel the same way. But you've got to think cool and precise right now. We both do or we're dead." He eased into what he wanted to know, not wanting to blow it at a delicate moment like this. "You're pretty good with that M-16."

She accepted the fresh magazine he handed her and fed it into the rifle.

"The military gave defensive weapons training before sending me here," she replied vaguely. "There...is no turning back for me now, is there?"

"They already knew about you. Lansdale and I were going to warn you. That was good timing, you showing up back there."

"You told me what you would do. When I left his home, I chanced the drive to wait near the base. You attempted impossible odds but...there is something about you that inspires confidence.

There should be more people like you in the world to do what needs to be done. Now...there is one less."

She reached across and gently lifted one of Lansdale's hands, pressed it to her cheek for one brief moment and kissed her lover's soul goodbye for the last time, then Katrina Mozzhechkov turned in the front seat to stare out the windshield.

"They'll have the city corked tight in no time, if they haven't already," said Bolan. "A description of you and this car will be going out on the air right now. We'll have to find other transportation. You should come with me, Katrina. They'll kill you if you stay in Kabul."

He braked the Tatra along a dark stretch in the suburbs where clusters of trees provided a good enough hiding spot for the car at least until dawn.

"You are right, of course." She nodded and Bolan could see she was grappling with inner demons.

But he had to know.

"Before we go any further, Katrina, you've got to tell me. Lansdale spoke to you when you helped him into the back seat right before he died, didn't he? I've got to know what he said."

She turned to eye him with open speculation.

"You ask me to trust you, Mack Bolan. Do you trust me?"

"Countless lives are at stake, Katrina. Every second counts. I trust you, yes."

"He spoke the name of a town. Parachinar."

Bolan nodded, his mental intel file clicking up the essentials.

"On the Pakistan border. A militia garrison is stationed there. That would be the place, all right. It would do them fine."

"Is it . . . the Devil's Rain?" she asked quietly.

"What do you know about that?" Bolan asked quickly, reaching forward to grab her by the shoulders.

"Only that you asked me about those words when we first met . . . and I know in my heart it is the reason my man is dead." She made a decision and changed the way she looked at him. "We have been through too much together this night, you and I, for us not to trust each other."

"We'll travel to Charikar," he told her. "But we'll have to find another vehicle first. I'll hotwire one. Our biggest problem will be Soviet patrols."

"There are several ways to get from Kabul to Charikar," the Russian woman told him. "I know them all. There is one way; it will be several hours longer but the patrols will overlook it. Soviet patrols have attempted to secure it in the past and have never been seen or heard from again."

Bolan considered.

Tarik Khan's force would pull away from their position in the foothills near Kabul the instant they received word of the Executioner's blitz on the Soviet high command. The *mujahedeen* would wait in Charikar, as Tarik Khan had promised, for word from Bolan on the site where a target named Vou-kelitch prepared a mass horror called the Devil's Rain.

Parachinar.

That is where the big hit would go down.

If Bolan could trust Katrina Mozzhechkov, a person he wanted to trust, a human being he liked already, probably too much.

A lot of what would happen from here on in depended on Lansdale's dying word as relayed by this woman. Lansdale had trusted her, true, but one fact could not be denied no matter how positively Bolan reacted to the woman.

Lansdale was dead.

Bolan would trust Katrina, sure.

Up to a point.

Far more, though, he would trust his own instincts and combat prowess to keep him alive to the payoff of this mission.

He would shake this hell to its very foundations.

9

"I say we do not trust the woman," Alja Malikyar opined when asked.

Bolan crouched with Alja and Tarik Khan around the smoldering embers of the morning cooking fire.

The three men sipped coffee sweetened with peppermint from tin cups.

Bolan and Katrina had reached Charikar an hour before dawn in the third hotwired vehicle Bolan had "appropriated" to get them there following Katrina's directions.

Tarik Khan and his men had welcomed Bolan warmly but they had viewed the woman with undisguised suspicion from the beginning.

Bolan had grabbed a ninety-minute catnap once he made sure Katrina was safely ensconced in the temporary *mujahedeen* camp. Tarik Khan arranged for her accommodation out of deference to Bolan.

The catnap proved more than sufficient to recharge Bolan's batteries and now, at 0900 hours, he was discussing what he had learned last night and what they must do next if they had any hope at all of stopping the Devil's Rain before it began.

Tarik Khan had changed from his gaudy embroi-dered vest into garb that matched that of his men, the *patu*, a thin wool blanket that serves Afghans as shawl, coat, bed cover and prayer mat.

The *mujahedeen malik* had asked his second-in-command for input after hearing Bolan's precise account of last night's events in Kabul and of agent Lansdale's dying message via the woman.

Bolan could see *malik* Tarik Khan weighing Al-ja's thoughts on the matter. He spoke to counter them.

"If the Russians are developing the Devil's Rain at Parachinar and if we get there in time to stop them, then Katrina Mozzhechkov is responsible for saving the lives of untold thousands of your people, Tarik Khan."

"And if she is a Soviet spy?" Alja asked. "If she relays only information the Russians wished the man, Lansdale, and us, to have? The woman could be leading us to a massacre!"

Bolan played the card that had swayed his deci-sion.

"And what choice do we have?" he asked both men. "I say we hit Parachinar. I will bear full re-sponsibility for the woman until she is vindicated or condemned by what happens when we reach the fort."

The *malik* nodded, absorbing both points of view. At last the guerrilla leader spoke.

"Very well, *kuvii* Bolan, the woman shall accompany us. We begin the march at dusk. But you must realize the Russian woman is our mortal enemy and will be considered as such by my men. And by myself until she has proved herself. It can be no other way."

"As long as she isn't harmed," Bolan said, trying not to make it sound like a threat, only a statement of fact and condition, out of respect to the *mujahedeen* leader.

Tarik Khan nodded.

"So it shall be, *kuvii* Bolan. You have my word."

The village consisted of a motley collection of weathered-wood houses propped up by long poles.

The day had started shortly after dawn with prayers. The settlement had no electricity, no running water, no telephone; a single lantern provided all the light in the hut where Bolan had slept.

He had observed few signs of modern life: Soviet weapons and a few portable radios.

Bolan and the men had eaten of the traditionally hearty Afghan morning meal: chicken, mutton, bread, grapes and yogurt, before most of the villagers left to tend their crops and sheep as if a war did not rage around them.

Social life in the Afghan countryside is dictated by ancient feudal patterns. The Afghans are a diverse people including both Pashto speakers and Dari speakers; several disparate sects of Muslims; political leaders who like the way Iran is governed and would like the same for Afghanistan; and tribes

that have always hated each other over blood feuds
that have endured for centuries.

Though the differences between such groups are
dramatic, their one unifying aspect is the ancient
Afghan code of behavior known as *pushtanwalli*,
characterized by clear-cut obligations of hospitality
to travelers and fugitives, revenge against enemies
of tribe and family and adherence to manly
courage.

The most important part of this code is *mel-
masua*, which deals with hospitality. And so Tarik
Khan's force was given shelter by a tribe other than
its own.

Bolan felt restless to move on but appreciated the
necessity of a force the size of Tarik Khan's traveling only at night.

The ranks of the *mujahedeen* had swollen to
nearly thirty men since Bolan and Tarik Khan had
parted last night outside Kabul. The guerrilla attack
force comprised the full spectrum of Afghan society, from former white-collar professionals to
farmers and herdsmen.

The local *jukiabkr*, the leader of the village coun-
cil, and his tribe, ignored Tarik Khan's group. That
appeared to be okay with the *malik*'s group, the
clear-eyed assault force Bolan would be working
with.

The *jukiabkr*, a barrel-chested man with a
handlebar mustache, seemed to live on hashish, like
so many of the Afghan hill people. Right after

morning prayers Bolan saw the guy take shavings from a block of the resinous drug and smoke it in a water pipe. Bolan saw the *jukiabkr* the rest of the day smoking his hash mixed with tobacco and rolled into cigarettes.

Bolan would feel damn glad to be out of here.

The American ached for action and cursed the slow pace of the sun's progress across the sky.

Katrina stepped up to stand beside him as he stood gazing out over the ruggedly beautiful countryside from an overlook near the outskirts of the village.

"I do not wish to be a burden," she began. "I can feel the hatred in their eyes when they look my way."

Bolan offered her a cigarette but she declined.

"You're Russian. You've got to expect it."

"I expect it. I was a good Russian soldier, you see." Tense, she worried her lower lip between her teeth. "What happened between. . .the man Lansdale and myself. . .it had nothing to do with his work. It is right that you should understand this. At first, yes, he met me through Captain Zhegolov when he had the gall to impersonate a Russian officer and attend a dinner party at a general's home."

Some of the tension left and the corners of her mouth tipped in a bittersweet smile.

"I think I fell in love with him at that moment, and when he contacted me later and asked for a dinner engagement I knew the attraction was mutual. From there an attachment blossomed between us, a beautiful thing.

"When he told me who and what he really was it was after we had fallen in love and he trusted me enough to tell me. I told him then I could not betray the position of trust I had been put in. I realize now how they must have learned about me. Captain Zhegolov was one of his informers but even this I was never told. His work, my work, had no place between us. I cannot explain it."

"You don't have to. He felt the same way about you. No one can judge what you two had."

"And now that I have no choice, now that I cannot return, I worry about my family in Russia more than ever, and yet I feel a freedom almost as great as love itself. Do you understand this? And yet I am not free of what has happened, of my fate. . . of the life I carry in my womb."

"Your family may be all right," Bolan said. "For now that's all you can go on. I have many connections, Katrina. Some in Russia. We'll do what we can for them."

"I will accept what help you can give," she said, gazing at the Executioner, "but seeing one's love killed the way I did. . . I don't know what to think, what to feel, but I know I must do something to . . . after my acceptance and part in what my country is doing here."

"You're right about one thing, Katrina. You

don't know what to think. Not this soon after last night. You may feel normal in some ways, but believe me, you are in shock from what you witnessed and what you were called on to do. You're tough enough to stay hard, I can see that, but call off making any decisions, okay? You owe it to the new life inside you.''

"Do I owe his child a coward for a mother?" she asked, and did not wait for his response but touched his arm with fingertips that last night had triggered death from a blazing M-16, but right now transmitted the human touch, nothing sexual, not anything except caring. "The loyalty I felt to my country. . . I now feel for his memory. That is how it is. Thank you for listening to a woman analyze her soul aloud, Mack Bolan. And for not judging."

He could say nothing to that. He watched her turn and walk away.

The village seemed nearly deserted during the day except for Tarik Khan's men who lounged about in attitudes of anticipation; the "hurry up and wait" syndrome of all military operations everywhere, even among guerrillas such as these.

Bolan preferred working alone or with only a small, select team. He had lost too many allies, from his early death squad days against the Mafia when he had enlisted the ill-fated members of his Nam combat team, right up to that terrible moment when April stopped a bullet meant for him.

Bolan felt he would give anything to have that one

moment repeated so he could know the bullet was coming and take it instead of her. He found himself realizing more and more as time put distance between *now* and *then* that the bullet that killed April had killed a part of Mack Bolan, too.

He still had friends he cared about as human beings, most of them hellgrounders who had served with him in one capacity or another during the Executioner's bloody miles, but Bolan recognized that something within himself had changed, possibly disappeared forever, though he hoped not.

A sense of *humanness*, yeah, that was it. The human fighting machine had risked everything more than once, pulling off the impossible over and over again in battlefields around the world, stopping the cannibals.

For love.

It might sound corny but people were the only thing that really mattered, Bolan knew; what they could aspire to and become and the promise of a better world someday, somehow, every time lovers touched. April Rose had been all of that and more to Mack Samuel Bolan, and when she died...yeah, something real big in the big guy named Bolan died, too, and all life held for him now was the fight itself.

But, bet on it, when it came to stopping cannibals and something called the Devil's Rain, this guy's war everlasting was reward enough.

10

The sun eased into the western horizon, splashing the rugged beauty of snowcapped mountains a warm red.

Bolan crouched, checking his weapons and gear prior to moving out.

Tarik Khan, Alja and the village *jukiabkr* approached him shortly after the traditionally light evening meal of flat bread and tea.

Bolan quelled an immediate irritation at the arrogance with which the *jukiabkr* carried himself.

"It seems a Soviet convoy has chosen to camp for the night two kilometers from here," Tarik Khan told Bolan. "Trouble with one of their vehicles."

"Let them be," Bolan growled. "Let's move out. Our fight with the Russians is elsewhere."

"I, uh, quite agree. Unfortunately, it is the request of our host, the *jukiabkr*, and is as such a demand, that my force assist his in attacking the Soviet camp. To refuse would be interpreted as a direct insult after the hospitality they have extended us."

Bolan glanced at the *jukiabkr*. The village leader

returned a glare of pointed rudeness but said nothing.

"Does he speak English?"

"No, but I am compelled to render a faithful translation of all you say."

"Fine. Have you explained to him the importance of our mission?"

Alja spoke up before his commander could reply.

"I say we aid the *jukiabkr*. Are not the Russians to be slaughtered wherever we find them when they do not expect us? The reason these soldiers risk camping in this area at all and do not push on with their remaining vehicles is that they believe this village to be secure. We can take them in an hour's time and easily be on our way. Allah has placed these Russian pigs before us to be slaughtered in the holy name of Islam. Can we turn our backs on the will of Allah?"

Bolan delivered a chilled glare.

"Alja Malikyar, you are a brother in arms and a brave man in the field of combat, but your zealousness will get you killed."

"Then that, too, is Allah's will," the feisty hill fighter shot back. "I live to slay my enemy in His name and so shall I die."

Tarik Khan looked to Bolan.

"You see how it is, my friend. Many of my men feel this way."

"I thought you were in command of this force, Tarik Khan."

"I am. But we speak now, *kuvii* Bolan, of religion and tradition and the power they have to shape a man's destiny, something your Western cultures have forgotten."

The *jukiabkr* groused a belligerent demand in Pashto, the language in which Tarik Khan responded before translating for Bolan.

"He wants to know if we, you and I, are with him. I have told the *jukiabkr* that I must discuss the matter with you."

"I appreciate that. And now that we've discussed it?"

"Do you appreciate my predicament, *kuvii* Bolan? Allah directs my fate, too. I have misgivings but it can be no other way in light of who and what I and my people are."

Bolan had not come all this distance to sacrifice the mission to these people's religious fervor. He had come to help, but he could not help them with themselves. But this was still his mission as well as theirs, and if they did not consider the mission objective he would have to for them. He restrained his irritation and a strong urge to punch Hash Breath in the mouth.

He said to Tarik Khan, "You have surely noted the fogged mental condition of the *jukiabkr*. His men are in no better shape and they've been working in the fields all day. If we go into battle with them, it will be suicide for too many of your men no matter how good they are, and will cost us manpower we need to accomplish our objective."

He refrained from mentioning details and Parachinar and hoped Tarik Khan and his men had done the same.

"This is a proud but foolish tribe," Tarik Khan explained to Bolan. "They would never allow us to do their fighting for them."

The village leader snarled an impatient demand that needed no translation.

Bolan resigned himself to the only possible course open to him if he wanted to salvage any hope at all for the Devil's Rain hit.

"Tell him I'm in," Bolan told Tarik Khan. "Advise him of my specialties; I have explosives. Tell the *jukiabkr* that I can infiltrate the Russians' encampment, then you and his *mujahedeen* can swoop in for the mop-up. With the damage I can do, that could cut our losses to nothing. If we come in blazing, those soldiers could defend their position and call in air support, which would take only minutes to arrive. We've got to level them with one decisive strike."

"You are right, of course," Tarik Khan said, nodding.

He proceeded to translate Bolan's words to the *jukiabkr*.

The village leader listened, scoffed in contempt, then turned and stalked away.

Alja Malikyar shook his head, watching the *jukiabkr* return to a cluster of his own men.

"It is indeed unfortunate we must ally ourselves

with such unwashed creatures. I beseech your for-
giveness, *malik* Tarik Khan, for so disrespectfully
voicing my thoughts moments ago.''

"What did Hash Breath just say?" Bolan asked.

Tarik Khan paused.

"He said he would not take orders from an infidel such as yourself. He will allow you to do as
you suggest, but he is the one who will direct his
men when to attack the Soviet convoy whether you
have finished your placing of explosives or not. He
said you will not live out this night.''

LIEUTENANT JOSEF BUCHEKSKY wondered if he had
not made a grave error in judgment in ordering the
fifteen-man unit under his command to encircle
their vehicles—two BTR-40s, the GAZ tanker that
had thrown a rod and the armored personnel carrier
that had carried troops to guard the precious fuel
delivered to the outpost in distant Baghlan to the
north.

A hundred kilometers from Kabul and they break
down!

Bucheksky had ordered his men to camp here for
the night.

Sergeant Iamskoy, the group's ranking noncom,
immediately set up security measures within the
circle of vehicles, which reminded the lieutenant
of a scene he had once seen in a German-made,
government-approved film about the American
west; the twenty-three-year-old officer nursed a

fascination with American history that he tactfully refrained from mentioning to those with whom he served.

Bucheksky fired a cigarette and tried to let the peacefulness of the night relax him. A man felt enveloped by the elements here in the wilderness, he thought, which is as a man should feel. Then he reprimanded himself for entertaining such useless notions and returned his attention to the problem at hand.

Bucheksky had been in Afghanistan only a month and had yet to see combat.

He recognized the queasiness in his stomach as fear.

We should have pushed on, he thought for the hundredth time since the gloom of night had descended across this desolate valley less than an hour ago.

Camping here had seemed the right thing to do at the time, in the bright light of day. The only village nearby had never shown signs of antigovernment activity, had seemed friendly as some of the mountain tribes appeared to be; the sensible ones, thought Bucheksky.

The "highway" cutting through the valley toward Kabul, so badly in need of repair, was quite another matter and on further reflection the young officer decided he had made the right decision, especially taking into account the trouble in the capital last night that officers in the field had been notified of: a strike at the very heart of the high command.

There were no actual details and it was too soon to tell if the assault had been an isolated incident. The *mujahedeen* had never struck at the nation's capital before; a suicide fringe could be responsible. Or was this the beginning of an orchestrated counteroffensive by a united Muslim front?

The lieutenant considered himself a man of letters marred by a personality flaw he had yet to overcome; he had the sensibilities of an artist but had not developed a strength of conviction necessary to achieve independence of thought and action—and he knew it.

Bucheksky's father was a retired general and upon Josef's completing the state-required formal education there had been no question that he would follow in his father's and grandfather's footsteps to officers' training school and a career in the military service of Russia.

At least Bucheksky had never questioned it and here he was, a man who knew he would one day pen the twentieth-century epic of his people, or so he hoped, and who had for the time being rationalized appeasing his father with the hope that a military career would at some not-too-distant point afford him the financial stability to subsidize such aspirations.

Though a loyal soldier of the Soviet Union, Bucheksky remained a man who loved American jazz and detective stories when he could find them. But where was he now? In some desolate, primitive country, learning nothing but fear; facing his own cowardice before a real world that he lied to himself he understood and could write about. . . .

Here stood Lieutenant Josef Bucheksky on his first true mission, though in reality it was nothing but a minor exercise and his superiors knew it, this routine accompanying of the fuel truck through a pacified countryside. But Bucheksky had read all too vividly the hostility in the eyes of every Afghan civilian they passed and the flutter in his stomach would not go away. Nor would the foreboding that he had made a mistake.

Sergeant Iamskoy strode over. The noncom had twenty-two years' experience on the lieutenant, yet no conflict had developed between them. The elder soldier had responded to something in Bucheksky and had sort of taken the younger man under his wing, though their exchanges recognized their respective ranks.

Bucheksky felt a sense of security and safety just knowing Iamskoy was here tonight.

"The sentries will be rotating every two hours, sir," the sergeant reported. "That will keep them fresh. Kabul will send out mechanics and parts first thing in the morning."

"But not tonight, eh?"

"This area—"

"Yes, I know, Sergeant. Friendly. Then I wonder why Kabul won't send us help tonight?"

"Probably don't want to spare any men after

what happened last night," the noncom opined. "I've got a feeling we're not being told the full story on that. I wonder why."

Bucheksky finished smoking his cigarette and flicked it into the darkness beyond the circle of vehicles. He watched the tiny red dot of the butt arc and for a minute sensed the presence of a breeze but there was no breeze. But the sensation was so momentary he dismissed it as nerves.

"When have we ever been told the whole truth, Sergeant?"

Iamskoy frowned.

"Excuse me for saying so, sir, but talk like that does not become an officer."

"Our civilians wait in endless lines for the barest necessities," Bucheksky went on, "and the only way a man can find security in a steady job is in military service. I sometimes think our country's expansionism has nothing to do with political ideology, Sergeant, but serves to save an economy that, if it fell, would mean many changes in our government at home. Then maybe we would have peace.

"But I suppose it is the soldier who always wants peace the most, is it not, for it is the soldier who is sent to fight and die when war comes. Why are we so far from home, Sergeant? Man to man. Why don't we all just march home? What would happen then? Would it be the end of the world?"

Iamskoy rested a hand on the younger man's arm.

"I do not hear your words. Speak no further. You

are Russian. We are soldiers. We serve our motherland. It is our duty."

At the instant Iamskoy spoke that last word, the world erupted with the fury of hell and Josef Bucheksky instinctively knew that his foreboding had been prophecy.

Explosions shattered reality from three of the vehicles across the encampment, balls of flame igniting the night.

11

Bolan had made a careful study of the Soviet encampment alongside the road and assessed its security as tight, formidable, set up by someone of seasoned field experience.

The outer perimeter consisted of four sentries, positioned a distance of fifty yards from one another outside the small camp, each holding an AK-47 as he patrolled a larger circumference, ten yards out from where the tanker, personnel carrier and two armored cars had been drawn into a circle.

The nightstalker made a third outer circle as he moved unnoticed to thoroughly reconnoiter and plan his one-man penetration of those defenses.

At the open spaces between each vehicle, inside the camp, stood another sentry.

Bolan discerned a Soviet officer who stood smoking a cigarette, staring out into the darkness. The man was unaware that close to sixty pairs of eyes from two separate groups were at that moment trained on him like a specimen under a microscope, from either side of this valley in which the Russians had been forced to spend the night.

Bolan counted sixteen soldiers down there, seven wrapped in sleeping bags on the ground in the center of the circle, no doubt resting up for their turn at standing guard. But Bolan knew the 50-to-16 odds were not overkill because those troopers were Soviet soldiers, among the very toughest in the world.

The thirty or so *mujahedeen* of Tarik Khan's force waited along the ridges and crests of the western wall of the small valley while twenty ragtag ruffians of the *jukiabkr* held the high ground to the east.

After both sides had been deployed, Bolan had left Tarik Khan's group on a southeasterly approach to the camp on the valley floor.

The penetration specialist had suppressed his misgivings about this hit and concentrated on a by-the-numbers infiltration between two of the outer sentries.

The only thing that mattered now was the success of the mission, which meant doing as much damage as he could and getting away without casualties to his own side.

When Bolan got past the patrolling sentries, he moved first to one of the BTR-40 armored cars.

He held some of the plastic explosive in his hands. He knelt silently before the hulking shadow of the war machine and wedged some death putty against the axle at the front tire.

The sentry posted between the BTR-40 and the

armored personnel carrier did not even blink when shadows shifted before his eyes a couple of paces away.

The night-hit expert in black proceeded to plant more timed explosives in the three other vehicles.

He went undetected during the two-and-a-half-minute operation.

When Bolan passed the juncture between the next BTR and the elongated shadows of the tanker, he noted through his NVD goggles that the officer had been joined by a tough-looking noncom.

Bolan caught enough of their exchange as he passed to remind the Man from Blood that these were human beings he had to kill tonight, not some targets in a game, the officer voicing a damn accurate assessment of the real reasons for the USSR's globe grabbing.

Bolan heard the noncom urge his officer to cool it. There seemed an almost father-son regard between the two. Then the nightkiller blocked such thoughts and continued with his work.

He paused until a sentry strolled past, and when the Executioner saw an opening he broke from the tanker, as stealthy as a wraith. For a heartbeat Bolan thought his presence had been discovered when the Russian flicked a cigarette butt that arced to within a foot of him.

The officer had watched it and Bolan thought he saw the man pause in his conversation with the noncom. The Executioner had remained still, fearing that the officer had sensed Bolan, but he guessed the officer decided it could only be the breeze or something and the Executioner got clear, past the sentries to several hundred yards away from where Tarik Khan's men waited.

Bolan flung himself in a forward dive to the valley floor one heartbeat before the plastique started ripping the night apart with hellfire behind him. After the last of the clustered explosions finished, gas tanks of the vehicles mushrooming golden balls of flame in the night sky, the nighthitter stood, gripped his MAC-10 in firing position and moved in.

The valley echoed with the unearthly shrieks of Allah's holy warriors as *mujahedeen* stormed down from either side of the valley to join the fray, each force reserving at least half of its men while the others rushed in firing weapons.

Chaos and confusion reigned within the circle of vehicles that had erupted into a circle of death and destruction.

WHEN THE FIRST RAPID SERIES of explosions rumbled from the near distance like approaching thunder, Katrina Mozzhechkov experienced stomach spasms that matched those rumbles of doom note for note.

She sat on a chair near the door of a vacant farmhouse. The occupants had left, the man to fight with the *mujahedeen*, his wife to wait somewhere with the other village women, shunning Katrina as they had all day.

Katrina felt afraid but she tried to fight her fear, to ride out the emotion, telling herself that because her moods had fluctuated so since last night, after what had happened to her lover, this fear would pass, too.

She feared also for the man known as the Executioner, and as she heard the faint secondary explosions, almost inaudible, she considered again what her fate among these people would be if Mack Bolan were killed in the raging battle or otherwise could not protect her.

He had strongly requested she remain in the village. She understood he did not want her exposed to unnecessary danger, knowing she carried a new life within her. But she had insisted on taking her chances anyway, until he explained that there would be no way possible she could survive.

He trusted Tarik Khan's men implicitly, but he feared the local men had probably already planned to kill her as an enemy of Allah and to claim it an enemy hit during the heat of the battle. Katrina knew the big American had to be right when she considered again the hatred with which she had been regarded all day in this strange, terrible place.

And so she agreed to stay behind, but as she heard those rumbles of war, Katrina Mozzhechkov felt many things: fear, anger, loss...and a frustration that would not go away; a need to do something, not sit here on the sidelines.

She had to prove herself.

To the unborn child within her.

To the memory of her lost lover.

And most of all to herself.

She stood, gripping the M-16 that Bolan had left her, and started toward the door.

THE FORCE OF THE EXPLODING CAB of the tanker pitched Sergeant Iamskoy into Lieutenant Bucheksky.

Bucheksky somehow registered the lucid thought, Thank God the tanker is empty! as he and the noncom toppled backward onto the ground toward the center of the circle of vehicles.

Dazed, the lieutenant started to his feet the instant they landed. He reached for his holstered side arm and realized Sergeant Iamskoy made no such similar effort.

Bucheksky looked, knowing what he would find, and fought to hold back the cry of panic and the bile that threatened to spew from his throat when he saw what remained of the man who had been like a father to him.

Sergeant Iamskoy's corpse lay draped across the officer's lower legs, the sergeant's back a charred, shredded ruin, the tunic ripped away, all visible flesh seared into puckered, smoldering horror around a dark hole where a chunk of flaming shrapnel had skewered him.

Bucheksky scrambled to his feet, the Tokarev

pistol in his fist. He crouched as he looked around frantically at the holocaust that had befallen his command: the screams of one man in flames razored the air, the soldier squealing as he rolled about on the ground. The stench of burned human flesh made Bucheksky nauseous. He saw the body of another soldier lying in an impossible position, the man's legs torn off at midthigh and nowhere to be seen; the man mercifully was dead or soon would be.

Flames licked the night sky as everything burned.

The soldiers in the center of the encampment stumbled to their feet, grabbing rifles with the confusion of men torn from deep sleep.

Bucheksky felt an odd surreal objectivity grip him. He somehow felt oddly removed from the sounds and terror of battle, and although part of it, still able to observe it all and know exactly what he should do. Survival instinct, he thought, as he flared into action. His training replaced fear now that the battle raged.

More gunfire poured down on the flaming camp from the slopes of the valley. Battle cries in Pashto accompanied the red winking of automatic gunfire as rounds whistled into the camp.

A soldier near Bucheksky pitched sideways when the left side of his skull exploded from the impact of an incoming round into a dark mist against the firelight.

The sentries on the outside perimeter held, falling

flat to the ground and firing auto bursts at the attacking waves of *mujahedeen*.

In the illumination from the fires, Bucheksky saw one of his soldiers lifted off the ground into a backward somersault as a bullet cored his face.

The lieutenant turned to shout something, anything, to his men who were now rushing to openings between the flaming vehicles, toward the attackers who had come within ten yards out there in the dark.

There would be no contacting Kabul by radio, Bucheksky knew; the explosions had effectively destroyed all his unit's communications equipment. He had heard no incoming missiles but how could the explosives have been planted without detection by his men?

Before Bucheksky could encourage his men he saw something. His eyes had almost missed it until he focused to see it again.

A shadow, a human shadow, darting past the glow of a flaming armored car.

Not a soldier! Bucheksky realized.

A big apparition in combat black was striding past the fires, pumping a mercy round into the flaming soldier who had somehow stayed alive and kept squealing until the specter freed the man's soul.

Bucheksky moved in that direction, pistol up, searching for the phantom.

Could one man have planted all these explosives?

Done all this damage? Who was this executioner of so many good soldiers? Bucheksky would stop him.

He saw the combat shadow again, too late. The specter tossed something that could only be a grenade and the ghost faded back into the night.

The young officer angled away from the melee of his men returning fire at the *mujahedeen*.

The grenade exploded with a ferocity that blasted apart one soldier and hurled three others aside like a child's discarded toys. Two of the men got dazedly to their feet, and the third shuddered in death throes where he fell.

Gunfire and grunts of hand-to-hand combat from outside the circle of flame peppered the night.

"Move out of the circle! Disperse! We're easy targets down here!" Bucheksky shouted to his men.

The crisp authority carried across the melee, the men toting their AKs out of the flickering ring of dying flames to confront their attackers.

Bucheksky fanned the night with his pistol. He cut into the direction where he guessed that the night-shadow would turn next if he continued the progression of his last two appearances.

The officer heard curses in Russian and Pashto all around him amid the noise of combat, but all that mattered to him at that instant was staying alive.

He sensed movement coming at him from his right, the opposite side from where he had guessed he would intercept the lone death-bringer in combat black.

Bucheksky crouched and tracked his pistol in the direction of the sound and glimpsed a *mujahedeen* guerrilla in traditional Afghan garb shouting something in Pashto and triggering off a burst of automatic fire in the lieutenant's direction.

The Russian officer dodged to the side in time and squeezed off one round from his Tokarev, the first time he had ever fired on a man.

The guerrilla caught the bullet through his open mouth in midscream; the slug blew away the back of his skull.

Bucheksky felt nothing except the urge to stay alive. He turned in the direction where he had expected to see the nightscorcher and realized as he turned that his luck had run out and so had his life.

The shadow in black dashed past Josef Bucheksky on his way to another point in the battle.

The young officer brought up his pistol as quickly as he could.

Without slowing the nightscorcher triggered a burst from an Ingram MAC-10 as he jogged past.

For twenty-three-year-old Josef Bucheksky, everything went black.

The Executioner shifted combat-cool eyes from the toppling body of the officer to survey the battle winding down around him.

The two *mujahedeen* forces had descended with a fury from higher ground upon the Russian encampment. The *jukiabkr* had held back the signal for his men to attack as Bolan had hoped he would until after the plastique had exploded.

AFTER PLANTING the puttylike charges, Bolan had held back as the *mujahedeen* delivered blistering salvos of autofire into the flaming camp during their charge to the valley floor from west and east.

Bolan had stayed well out of the softening-up fire. He had fired on the outside sentry to the north, canceling that man before the guy could find suitable cover.

In no time the *mujahedeen* had overrun and taken out the other three sentries, two of the troopers falling in brutal hand-to-hand combat with men of Tarik Khan's force.

Hash Breath and his boys chose to hold well back, Bolan had noted, though their spotty fire into the camp toppled another of the Soviet infantrymen inside the ring of fire.

Bolan had next heard the snap of a pistol shot almost lost beneath the mix of close-quarter warfare and glanced as a young Soviet officer drilled and killed Alja Malikyar with a well-placed shot through Alja's open, screaming mouth. Alja had foolishly rushed the officer, shouting zealous Islamic phrases as many other *mujahedeen* fighters did, except Alja shouted too soon.

Damn fool, Bolan had thought sourly. So Alja is with his beloved Mohammed. What a waste. Bolan had taken out the officer with a burst from the MAC-10 before moving on.

The third sentry had made the mistake of angling away from the flame light right into the thickest of the *jukiabkr*'s force where Hash Breath and some of his men had held the screaming soldier down on the ground and laughingly beat him to death with their rifle butts.

Bolan disciplined an urge to level those *mujahedeen*, but for once he had no choice in his allies in battle.

He catfooted back to the smoldering hulk of the wreck of the personnel carrier.

Three Russian soldiers remained alive, moving well away from one another in an attempt to secure cover that did not exist. They saw their executioner and tracked three AK-47s as one in his direction, but Bolan had the killing edge.

He delivered a fusillade of scything slugs that hammered two men, hurling them into the smoldering ruin of a BTR-40 where their dead flesh fried.

The Executioner drew a bead with his M-16 on the last soldier, just as that one bought it from a hail of bullets from Tarik Khan's assault rifle.

The last Soviet soldier flew backward to the ground in a wide-armed sprawl with a line of holes tracked left to right across his chest.

12

With the fading battle sounds came the hubbub of the *jukiabkr*'s men descending on the corpses like buzzards, stripping dead soldiers of everything from uniforms to weapons to money, mob-rule anarchy dominating the scene.

Bolan turned away in distaste. He slammed another magazine into his Ingram.

Tarik Khan did the same with his AK.

Bolan approached Tarik Khan's men, who were regrouped in subdued businesslike fashion, a striking contrast to the scavengers from the nearby village whom they regarded with contempt as they counted their own numbers.

"It seems the only loss we suffered was the unfortunate Alja, a noble man whose soul now knows a better place," Tarik Khan told Bolan. "My men and I thank you, *kuvii* Bolan, for the quick retribution you bestowed upon the infidel who took Alja's life. We shall move out at once to begin our march."

Bolan glanced over the *malik*'s shoulder.

The village *jukiabkr* strode toward them, flanked by two of his men who gripped their weapons, old

Lee-Enfields, with fingers on the triggers and tense eyes closely watching Bolan, Tarik Khan and the others.

The *jukiabkr* halted half a dozen paces from Bolan, as did his men, arrogantly, his belligerence nastier from the excitement of seeing bodies shredded and blood flowing.

The same as those cannibals who were about to torture Lansdale and enjoy it last night in Kabul, thought Bolan.

The *jukiabkr* snarled in Pashto, aiming his rifle at the ground. He did not have quite enough guts to raise it on Bolan. Yet. But recklessness shone in Hash Breath's glazed eyes.

Tarik Khan sensed Bolan tensing for a kill. The *mujahedeen* chief placed a hand upon Bolan's shoulder so as not to interfere with Bolan's response but to give the big guy reason to pause.

"Please, brother," he half-whispered to Bolan, his voice taut. "This is but one village, yes, but for you or one of my men to slay this man would result in a tribal feud that would do nothing but harm the cause of all *mujahedeen*."

Hash Breath snarled something with a vigorous nod in Bolan's direction.

The men with the *jukiabkr* inched out to each side until Bolan's glance stopped them.

Tarik Khan translated.

"He knows who you are, my friend. He knows you are wanted by the Soviets and your own people.

He demands that I assist him in killing you and turning in your head to the Russians for a reward. He can then blame you for tonight's attack and claim the reward offered for you.''

The *jukiabkr* did not like Tarik Khan speaking in English to the American. He snarled again and made a gesture with his rifle, though he still did not pull the weapon up anywhere near a firing position.

Bolan kept his eyes on Hash Breath.

''And what is your decision this time, *kuvii* Tarik Khan?''

''You should not have to ask, my friend. Some things are worth a blood feud, such as friendship between men like ourselves. We disagreed about tonight's action; this does not mean I no longer consider you my brother. These are not my brothers; their own tribe would be disgraced by them.''

The *jukiabkr* growled one more time, a single harsh grunt to build up his own courage and that of his two gunmen.

The confrontation crackled with tension.

''Tell this scumbag,'' Bolan said in precise, even tones, ''that unless he shows me his back right now, he and his two boys are dead meat. They've got five seconds.''

Tarik Khan's eyes smiled. He stepped away from Bolan but faced the other tribesmen to stand with his own rifle at the ready. He translated.

The *jukiabkr*'s mouth tightened, his eyes shot anger at Tarik Khan for having tipped his hand to the American when the *jukiabkr* thought he had the *malik* in line and expected cooperation.

Four seconds dragged by like an eternity to Tarik Khan. He caught a peripheral impression of the big American in blacksuit, like a statue, firm, unmoving, unstoppable, slit blue eyes like cold bits of ice, no fear of death.

The *jukiabkr* read those eyes, too.

The village leader turned abruptly and stalked off without a word, his men following him without hesitation.

The Executioner watched the *jukiabkr*'s retreat, not lowering his Ingram.

"You are wise not to have killed him since you did not have to," Tarik Khan said. "You are wise in most things, it would seem, *kuvii* Bolan. But enough talk. My men are ready. We begin the march."

"Enough talk," Bolan agreed. "Let's move out."

None of the locals attempted to stop Tarik Khan or the icy-eyed American and their men as the *malik*'s silent *mujahedeen* fell into a double file behind their leaders. They headed toward the village where the Russian woman was waiting, leaving the *jukiabkr*'s men to paw over dead Soviet soldiers.

Tarik Khan felt loathing from the *jukiabkr* and could sense his eyes burning holes into the *malik*'s back. Tarik Khan knew the village leader would not take lightly the disgrace he suffered in the showdown with Bolan.

The *jukiabkr* would not order his men to open

fire, for these were a cowardly lot. But Tarik Khan
had a slithering premonition that in some ways it
would have been better for this mission if Bolan had
killed the man he called Hash Breath, regardless of
the strife among mountain tribes such an act would
have caused. Tarik Khan's force could not afford
another delay if they hoped to stop the Devil's Rain
in time.

Before the war, Tarik Khan had lived in Mazar-i-
Sharif, near the Soviet border. He had long ago re-
conciled himself to the fact that he would never see
his hometown again. He no longer wanted to, knowing it could never be as he remembered it before in-
fidels from the north came to pillage, plunder and
rape, attacking the countryside in order to isolate
any resistance movement, setting fire to crops and
storage shelters. Settlements near the border had
been the first to feel the wrath of the Soviet invaders.

The fools, Tarik Khan thought once again; they
know nothing of the people they hoped to conquer or
of the power of Islam. The area had been evacuated,
true, but all survivors had united with other victims
of Soviet aggression to wage a *jihad*, a holy war to
the death, against these Russian pigs.

Tarik Khan had become their most powerful leader. He prayed to Allah, even as his *mujahedeen* commenced their withdrawal from this scene of
slaughter, that they would reach Parachinar in time
to attack the fort there. He hoped they could abort a
holocaust that would surpass the atrocities of the

Nazis or even the mass devastation these Russian invaders had already wrought upon Tarik Khan's beloved Afghanistan.

The *mujahedeen* leader knew that any faith at all he had in the success of this operation could only be placed in the hands of Allah, in the toughness and spirit of his men...and in the savage presence of an incredible human fighting machine, the American, Mack Bolan. The Executioner.

But time was running out.

They could already be too late.

13

Bolan and Tarik Khan's force pushed on relentlessly across hostile, cruel terrain.

The Executioner realized again what superb condition these men were in, the ceaseless march forward to reach Parachinar testing even his own stamina. This made him appreciate all the more the fact that Katrina Mozzhechkov kept pace at Bolan's side, never once lagging during the trek.

The nighttime journey was broken only at one point when a friendly tribe of *mujahedeen* assisted them with motorized transportation in an odd assortment of ancient vehicles over a stretch of mountains unpatrolled by the Russians.

This generous aid cut off what would have been several days of marching time; then another province began and the stealthy force continued on foot again, looking as if they would make it with perhaps an hour of darkness to spare.

Bolan could think of no recommendations to Tarik Khan regarding their security. The resistance leader commanded a damn tight ship: scouts with walkie-talkies were posted on each flank, several miles ahead and to the rear of the main group. Conversation was kept to a bare minimum the whole time even when they were being assisted by the friendlies.

At the end of that stretch of the trek, as Tarik Khan's men had debarked from the ragtag convoy to regroup and resume the march, Katrina had a few stolen moments with Bolan out of earshot of the others.

The Russian woman and Bolan had not spoken since the group briefly stopped at the village after the action near Charikar to pick her up and commence their march.

Bolan had been relieved to find her safe and waiting for them but had not missed the pain-racked look in her eyes. He had also observed an attitude of withdrawal about her that indicated a deep inner turmoil, but that did not deter her from a march that would have done in most American women and men Bolan knew.

His respect for Katrina made him care. He welcomed the chance to communicate with her and maybe help.

"We will reach Parachinar soon," she began. She gestured with the M-16 she toted. "I must do something. I can no longer sit by idly."

"Katrina, we've been over that."

"In the village during the attack on the convoy...I started toward that battle three separate times but I...I could not leave the hut. I was afraid."

"Any person would be."

"Are you afraid of death?"

"I risk it, I don't invite it. You're no coward, Katrina. I've seen you fight."

She nodded. "Thank you for understanding."

Then it came time to move out and resume silence during a stretch of the march through a somewhat populated area. Bolan had an uncomfortable hunch that he had not said the right thing at all to a woman who remained an unknown quantity, an enigma, who, yeah, could be one of the enemy, who could be a damn good actress playing a convincing part. But in any case Katrina Mozzhechkov was certainly a woman capable of anything.

Bolan and the *mujahedeen* reached the vicinity of the installation near Parachinar at 0400 hours.

The mountain fighters appeared little worse from the wear of the seven hours of constant movement.

The Executioner was wearing the traditional Afghan headgear that he had borrowed from Tarik Khan.

Tarik Khan chose a position along an irregular ridge of scattered spearmint bushes and mountain scrub trees; ideal for the placement of the heavy tripod machine guns that would be primarily for defense against Soviet air power, which the government forces would call for immediately after the assault began.

The first order of business, though, was to secure the area, which meant searching for mines. This was done by pressing the cheek to the ground to look for shallow depressions where the dirt had been scraped out to conceal a mine; it was a slow operation that could not be hurried, which proved a good thing.

Bolan himself led the exercise and after a few minutes of careful probing, he used wire cutters to defuse the first Russian explosive.

The *mujahedeen* also found two mines in the vicinity. They used sticks and twigs to carefully probe and gently push away the dirt until the mines could be safely lifted out.

"The area for miles around the fort will be mined," Tarik Khan told Bolan. "These evil ones do not care whom they kill."

The *mujahedeen* leader deployed his men effectively along the ridge with a complete absence of any sound save the occasional soft clinking and clanking as missile launchers and heavy machine guns were positioned.

"Come," Tarik Khan told Bolan as preparations for the attack continued around them. "We shall observe our target together."

They crouched down at a cluster of shrubbery that offered an unobstructed view of the fort: a square white structure resembling the walled outposts Bolan remembered from films about the old French Foreign Legion outposts in the deserts of North Africa.

Thirty-foot cement walls rose sheer with brick

watchtowers at each corner. Six sentries in each, manning heavy machine guns, scanned the one approach to the fort, crossing fifty yards of flat terrain to a blacktopped two-lane road that bisected the scene from north to south.

Bolan saw a helicopter pad and maintenance area.

The fortress had been constructed on an open plain, the floor of a wide valley.

Occasional structures, private residences, dotted the two-lane at irregular intervals as did the dark shapes of clusters of trees.

The fortress, especially the ground at the outside base of the walls, was bright from high-intensity floodlights but the overall impression to Bolan as he scanned with NVD goggles through binoculars was of a world asleep, not in any particular hurry to wake up to the grim realities of another day.

There was no traffic along the road at this hour.

Bolan had sprawled belly down beside Tarik Khan. Both men lowered their binoculars.

"It is one of three fortresses along the highway," Tarik Khan informed him. "This road is one of the army's major supply routes. They know the country belongs to us at night."

"What is their number down there?"

"It changes as the Soviets order the militia redeployed about the country. They will be mostly Afghan regulars. General Voukelitch chooses an unimportant place for his work, much as a spider spins his web where the light of day will not reveal it.''

Bolan nodded.

''The spider's web is a trap and that could be a trap down there whether they know it or not. I've got to go in solo again, Tarik Khan. If I can destroy the laboratory where they make and store this Devil's Rain, the attack by you and your men could serve as the diversion I'll need to get clear.''

The guerrilla studied Bolan.

''After your work in Kabul I would say it is the way you work best and it is for your abilities that I chose to summon you. There will be much danger for you but you will not be up against Russian soldiers. The militia is made up of untrustworthy draftees who defect daily.'' Tarik Khan raised his binoculars again to study the fort and its environs. ''The landing area must be my men's first target, of course. We are for the most part helpless against Soviet air power, but we will stop these before they get off the ground.''

''I see only helicopter gunships,'' Bolan noted. ''They'll have MiGs here within minutes. I'm sure they have a landing strip not far from here.''

''They do,'' the guerrilla said with a nod, ''but we still have time to operate. They hope to control too much territory with too little.''

Bolan knew the Soviets fought their war here on the cheap, figuring they had time on their side, and they were probably right. Only two percent of

Soviet defense spending goes to waging the Afghanistan war; only six percent of their army divisions are deployed in Afghanistan. As for their Kabul-regime allies, Tarik Khan had hit the nail on the head: those kidnapped into military service by an occupying invasion force rarely make good soldiers.

Bolan went through a last-minute check of his weapons and equipment.

"Give me ninety minutes, then hit them with everything you've got. Unless you hear fireworks from down there any time before then, which will mean I'm in trouble and need all the firepower I can get."

They synchronized their watches.

Time to move out.

Time to *do* it.

Bolan and Tarik Khan drew back from the ridge and stood to exchange the traditional handshake of farewell.

"Good luck, brother," the *mujahedeen* leader grunted solemnly. "May Allah guide you on the right path. And may we meet at the end of this battle. Our cause is just. Allah is with us."

"Live large, *malik* Tarik Khan," Bolan acknowledged, and he turned to say goodbye to Katrina Mozzhechkov.

The Russian woman had remained at his side until he and Tarik Khan had bellied to the ridge to reconnoiter.

She was nowhere in sight and Bolan cursed inside when he realized it.

Katrina was gone.

14

General Pytyr Voukelitch, KGB, studied the Afghan in hospital whites who sat handcuffed to a bed.

"A high fever was the only symptom he showed and it passed of its own accord within days," Dr. Golodkin, head of the technical staff, reported in Russian to his superior. "This man is now perfectly healthy."

The figure in the bed looked fearfully from one Russian towering over him to the other, unable to understand their language but somehow sensing his own existence was at stake.

"Were the others exposed at the same time as this one?" Voukelitch demanded.

"Dead, comrade General, but if the implementation of the, er, program hinges only on determining the intervals at which the solution should be spread, I would conservatively estimate the period of effectiveness at six weeks, based on these experiments. Is that what you need to know?"

The KGB commander stalked toward the door of the sterile room.

"It is. You have done well, comrade Doctor. Your services will be amply rewarded."

"Discreetly, I trust. Uh, what about this one?"

Voukelitch did not pause. He stepped from the room.

"Kill him, of course."

Voukelitch closed the door behind him and returned to his office at this outpost fifteen kilometers from Parachinar, accompanied as always by a uniformed bodyguard.

Major Ghazi, commandant of this Afghan garrison, waited for Voukelitch as the general had instructed him to in the office that had belonged to Ghazi before the KGB man arrived with orders placing Ghazi and his command at Voukelitch's disposal.

At his superior's entrance, Ghazi rose abruptly from the chair that faced the office desk.

Voukelitch strode to the liquor cabinet camouflaged behind a fake bookcase and spoke as he poured them each a shot of vodka.

"It is done, Major." Voukelitch handed the Afghan a shot glass and hoisted his own. "Operation Devil's Rain will commence with the first light of dawn."

They clinked glasses and downed the shots.

The Afghan chuckled without humor. A sound from the grave.

"You have outdone yourself, General Voukelitch. I had heard of your ingenious strategies in the

Panjir Valley during last winter's offensive. If I may say so, sir, this surpasses even that. It has been my privilege to be associated with a man of your vision."

Fawning pig, thought Voukelitch, though his pride basked in the compliment. He poured himself another shot without offering one to the Afghan officer, then replaced the bottle and glasses in their hiding place and returned to the desk.

The counterinsurgent operation that Ghazi spoke of concerned—for it was still being used—the air drop from helicopters of camouflaged antipersonnel mines and booby-trapped toys, usually small red trucks, designed not to kill but to injure, blowing off hands.

In this way guerrilla fighters would be demobilized while they transported and attended the victims—in the case of the "toy" bombs, almost always children—who would most likely die anyway from gangrene after days or weeks of atrocious suffering. The objective was to further depress and demoralize those who must watch the victims die.

Voukelitch, who at forty-seven had the physical condition of a man twenty years younger, held the opinion that all is indeed fair in war; to attain the goal, to win, was all that mattered.

To General Voukelitch, morality was but an invention of the weak to defend themselves.

He placed a Turkish cigarette into his onyx holder.

"What word from Kabul?" he asked Ghazi.

"Things are coming in piece by piece," the army major reported. "I have beefed up security. Early last night a convoy was massacred near Charikar."

"That area is secured."

"Uh, so Kabul thought. As you know, comrade General—"

"Yes, yes, of course, the situation is still far too fluid. Kabul believes this to be an orchestrated offensive then, is that it?"

"So it would appear."

"And yet it troubles me in particular, coming so close as it does to the implementation of Operation Devil's Rain." Voukelitch thought aloud through a blue-gray cloud of exhaled smoke. "The man Lansdale, the CIA agent, could well have been on to us and what we have been up to here these past four months."

"The man is dead, sir."

"True, but you had better triple your security measures, Major, and not only in preparation for possible attack from those savages. Whoever helped Lansdale to escape from the base at Kabul. . . . If Lansdale knew about us, it is most likely his allies now possess the information as well. All too likely."

"And you suspect someone other than the *mujahedeen*?"

"It could very well be."

"But who?"

"That is my concern, Major. Yours is to see that

this installation is impenetrable to attack. Operation Devil's Rain will not be delayed or sabotaged."

"Perhaps we should request reinforcements."

"That is a very bad idea, Major. Have I not repeatedly stressed the sensitivity of this project? There are members of the Central Committee and the General Staff who are not aware of the work that has gone on in the laboratory facility constructed here."

"Of course, comrade General, of course. A very bad idea."

"A far better one, Major, would be for you to personally see to increasing security measures immediately."

Ghazi again got abruptly to his feet to deliver a crisp salute.

"But of course, comrade General. I will see to it."

Voukelitch did not bother returning the salute.

"See that you do, Major. That will be all."

Ghazi turned and exited the office.

Voukelitch waited five minutes in silence, doing nothing but thinking, to insure that Ghazi would not return with some follow-up question.

The KGB man smoked another cigarette in the interim. When he felt certain he would not be disturbed, most of the base asleep at this hour in any event, he leaned forward and depressed a hidden buzzer he had installed on the underside of the desk since taking over this office.

A side door opened and Voukelitch's bodyguard entered, armed with a holstered pistol and a shoulder-strapped submachine gun.

"Yes, my General?"

"What have you learned, Corporal Fet?"

"I, uh, socialized with the CQ staff in the orderly room while you spoke alone with Major Ghazi," the Soviet soldier reported promptly. "Major Ghazi has done an admirable job in increasing security measures."

"Corporal" Fet was in fact a KGB agent, transferred to Ghazi's command as one of the regular Soviet liaison months before Voukelitch's arrival and the Devil's Rain project. Fet had seemed a random choice by Voukelitch as his bodyguard from the ranks, the perfect spy, a means by which Voukelitch could double-check on the camp CO's activities.

"Very good. Please lock the hallway door, Corporal."

The two men played out their roles in Fet's deception even in private.

"Yes, sir."

Fet locked the door and returned to stand before Voukelitch's desk.

"And our...other business?" Voukelitch inquired in a lower voice.

He had the office searched daily by Fet for hidden microphones, but one could never be too sure.

"Your pilot returned with a...passenger less

than thirty minutes ago,'' Fet replied in the same lowered voice. "The man awaits you now at the appointed spot.''

Voukelitch pocketed his cigarette holder, stood from his desk chair and started toward the door by which Fet had entered. "Excellent. We will leave as discreetly as possible, though no one will attempt to stop us.''

Fet moved to the door.

"It is good that we hurry, sir. The pilot told me that in addition to the goods...the *jukiabkr* has something vital to tell you.''

Voukelitch paused before the door. He unholstered his own pistol, checked it, reholstered it and nodded for Fet to open the door.

"Very well, Corporal. We are on our way. It is a busy night and far from over.''

Voukelitch and Fet exited the building via a side door. A sleek ZIL limousine stood waiting beside the building. Corporal Fet held open the door for the general, then moved around to the driver's seat.

Neither man spoke as the officer's car cleared through the well-guarded main-gate of the fort without being stopped, into the pitch-dark night.

Voukelitch considered again the advisability of liquidating Fet when this mission ended, since only Fet knew the true extent of the general's dealings in and around Parachinar.

The Devil's Rain operation was far more than strategical genocide in much the same way as the

KGB itself was far more than merely the security and terrorist arm of the USSR.

In fact, Pytyr Voukelitch and the inner core of the KGB had been exploiting the very capitalistic potentials of their far-flung organization's activities for years.

The military strategy of blanketing the Panjir Valley, the Khyber Pass and other vital areas with Devil's Rain was but a cover for its real value to General Voukelitch.

Other countries, Third World mainly, would pay dearly for the secret ingredients of the Rain and there was the "other business," one of the reasons he ventured out at night in the bulletproofed ZIL, though Ghazi had assured Voukelitch countless times that the vicinity was safe even at night.

Voukelitch had earlier that evening dispatched a Hind helicopter to a village in the relatively distant Charikar region to bring back the village *jukiabkr*.

During the past four months the man had served as an excellent source of hashish, which Voukelitch channeled on to the next link in the chain via KGB channels for his share of the considerable profits the drug brought from both Western countries and, more increasingly of late, from the Soviet Union herself. This pleased Voukelitch; it would be easier to make money closer to home and his cut would be larger.

He fitted another cigarette into his holder and lit it, reaching his decision.

No, he would not kill Fet. Not yet, he decided.

With the Devil's Rain ready to fall, Voukelitch reasoned that the first order of business would be to cancel out the *jukiabkr*.

Voukelitch expected to be moving on within days; dealings with the Afghan peasant would no longer be feasible and the man could hardly be allowed to live to tell others that he had wholesaled hashish in quantity to a Russian officer.

The whole of the KGB was impossible to control and there were elements, the naive, the idealists, who would have Voukelitch sent to the gulag if the activities of him and his cohorts ever came to light. No, he decided, the *jukiabkr* had expended his usefulness. Tonight he would die, and for that Voukelitch would need Fet.

The ZIL traveled at a snappy speed along the well-maintained road toward Parachinar, the limousine's headlights piercing the night like fingers pointing the way.

Voukelitch's mind jumped ahead in anticipation of what would happen after his rendezvous with the *jukiabkr*.

Until not too many years ago, prostitution in Muslim Afghanistan had been punishable by death—and probably still was among the mountain tribes, Voukelitch reflected—and things had not got much better.

The world's oldest profession was conspicuous by its absence in this nation of religious fundamentalism...except for the "safe houses" established by the Soviet command for the chosen among its ranks. Parachinar had not rated such a place until Voukelitch insisted on and supervised the start of one on the outskirts of town.

Voukelitch had long ago resigned himself to the fact that human relations only complicated and detracted from the quest for power that was his true lust. Yet he had the hungers of any man, more than most, he sometimes thought, when the money had been paid, the flesh owned, the control of another absolute.

He had been visiting the "house" every other night for the past four months, though he did not consider it an obsession. The general restricted his indulgences to those times when he was not needed in the laboratory at the base, when everything was running smoothly, as now; not like the deceased Colonel Uttkin, whom Voukelitch had considered a sadist well disposed of.

First, though, he must deal with the *jukiabkr*. The general knew he must learn what important information the unwashed savage claimed to have. Voukelitch despised the man as he did all of these Koran-thumping nitwits, but it could be significant that this *jukiabkr* hailed from a village in the vicinity of last night's massacre.

Everything was in place, everything moving smoothly ahead, all of Voukelitch's plans about to be realized. There was even bought flesh to lose himself in and still be back at the base in time for the first takeoff of a flight bearing the Devil's Rain. Yet, and he did not know why it irritated him, a premonition needled his subconscious that something was about to go wrong and there was nothing he could do about it.

General Pytyr Voukelitch had never experienced such a premonition in years of KGB work.

He tried to occupy his mind with thoughts of the whore waiting for him in the "house," of the things he would pay her to do to him.

But the premonition would not go away.

15

Katrina Mozzhechkov stood at the side of the road and watched the headlights draw near from the direction of the army fort two kilometers away.

She wore the khaki field outfit she had worn since the night before in Kabul when she had dealt herself into this thing. In some ways it seemed so long ago, and yet the death, before her eyes, of the man she loved would be seared into her soul forever. But never with the pain of now when it burned into her mind like a branding iron.

Katrina knew something of General Pytyr Voukelitch, the man she hoped would be a passenger in the approaching vehicle.

She gambled it would be he, though the hopeless odds that it would not be struck her anew. But this would be her first step in realizing the only thing that mattered since the instant her lover had died.

She drew strength only from a consuming need to somehow make all this mean something, especially the death of a good man named Lansdale whose seed she carried. The only way it could mean anything to Katrina Mozzhechkov was if it spurred her into righting at least some of the wrongs her country had wrought here in Afghanistan. She hoped that in the process she could redeem herself even if she died, because that, too, would have been worth it.

The approaching car was not near enough for the headlights to make her visible to its occupants but it would be in a matter of seconds.

She tried to strike a pose that she thought was provocative to male eyes, but realized she only looked foolish. Such posing had always seemed so superfluous to her; she had never been a flirt, though she knew she was not unattractive. She decided to stand naturally, without affectation.

The headlight beams embraced her. An officer's car. The vehicle reduced its speed but kept coming.

Katrina had known nothing of the Devil's Rain until the American, Bolan, brought her the realization that, whatever it was, it had caused her lover's death. Now that she knew where the Devil's Rain was, at that fort outside Parachinar, even if that was all she knew about it, at least she possessed knowledge that gave her an edge, an *inside* edge. It was a chance even the *mujahedeen*, even the American, did not possess to destroy whatever her government's army had here that had caused her man's death.

She would use the edge.

It would be Lansdale's legacy, too, and it *would* mean something because even if she sacrificed her life, Katrina Mozzhechkov would have redeemed her soul.

As Captain Zhegolov's typist at Soviet head-quarters in Kabul, Katrina routinely processed the monitoring of Soviet and Afghan army communiqués. She had processed the transfer of General Voukelitch to this obscure outpost four months earlier.

She recalled thinking it odd at the time, and odder still when Voukelitch requested additional security measures pertaining to something coded only by a number. Katrina had processed it with everything else and had long since forgotten it, never realizing an insignificant numeral lost in a long day's work months ago would lead her to this uninhabited stretch of road.

The officer's car stopped.

She approached it.

She had left the M-16 behind at the *mujahedeen* camp when she crept away half an hour before. She walked now with her shoulder-strap bag riding close to her side by her elbow. The purse contained, among other things, a 9mm Heckler & Koch VP70M automatic pistol.

She reached the car.

The driver's automatic window powered down.

"Yes, miss?" a Soviet soldier, a corporal, asked in Russian, snappy, a bit distracted but not impolite.

"I have had some misfortune." Katrina leaned to

speak toward a passenger she sensed in the tonneau.
"The gentleman I was with...was no gentleman.
We had an argument. He...left me stranded."

A voice from behind the driver said sympatheti-
cally, "The difficult road of true love?"

Katrina recognized the voice though she had only
heard General Voukelitch speak on one occasion
when he made a routine visit to Captain Zhegolov's
office. Voukelitch had a voice she would never forget because it made her skin crawl. And that is what
she remembered.

She remembered something else about the general
from office gossip and subsequent communiqués
monitored by Zhegolov's unit. And this is what had
brought her here, leaving the force of *mujahedeen*
and the Executioner behind; the cutting edge they
did not have: a knowledge of the general's compul-
sion.

It could be called nothing else, the officer's
penchant for out-of-the-ordinary sex that had come
to light when Voukelitch moved bureaucratic
heaven and earth to have an "officers' house"
opened and maintained in Parachinar.

Katrina knew what these "houses" really were
and it was something else about Voukelitch that
made her skin crawl, as had the routine intel reports
that the general visited his "house" every other
night.

She had not hoped for it to be this easy but she
knew that simply by virtue of being a woman she

could gain access to this man. She knew the address of his private whorehouse, if it came to that.

The plan had sprung full-blown to her; she would gain access to the garrison post and kill Voukelitch. Even if they captured her, as they most surely would, it would make the task of Bolan and the *mujahedeen* that much easier. But if she did somehow survive and managed to start a new life, then Katrina knew it would again be a life worth living.

"Hardly true love," she replied to the general. "May I trouble you gentlemen for a lift into town? I see you are headed in that direction."

"Of course," the voice purred from the tonneau. "Please join us. Miss Mozzhechkov, is it not?"

The one meeting and he remembered her too, which she had not counted on; or had Kabul issued a bulletin to apprehend her? Of course they had, Katrina realized with a chilly tremor down her spine. But she saw no options at this point but to follow through. She had her gun. She would not die without a fight.

Katrina entered the limousine.

The corporal shifted the ZIL into almost undetectable motion and continued on. The plush interior of the officer's car muffled the outside world.

"You are Captain Zhegolov's secretary, or at least you were when I visited the good captain several months ago," the general said, smiling emptily; his eyes said nothing. "I remember you, my dear, you see; a most charming daughter of the motherland."

"I am flattered, General. I likewise remember you."

She noticed a brief tight smile of his thin lips, there and gone.

"I did not know you had been transferred to the Parachinar area, my dear. I would have sought out your delightful company had I known." He extended a pack of Turkish cigarettes. "Smoke?"

"No, thank you."

He fitted one into his onyx holder and lit up. "Forgive me, it is my one unshakable vice."

"But of course, General."

Do it now! her mind screamed. Is it possible his work and vices have kept him so busy that he does not know I am wanted by Kabul?

Then she thought of where this could lead: onto the base, to the Devil's Rain, the further damage she could do, and she resisted the impulse to pull the gun from her purse and kill this pig right here and now.

She felt knotted up tight inside but hoped that Voukelitch, if he noticed it at all, would interpret it as her natural embarrassment at the situation she had invented to explain her presence here.

In what she hoped was a steady voice with just the right amount of throaty flirtatiousness, she said, "Actually, I have not been transferred. I am on a one-week furlough."

He regarded her through twin streams of smoke exhaled from his nostrils.

"A peculiar spot for a holiday, Parachinar."

Not an accusation, she thought, or is it? Is he playing me like a cat with a mouse?

"I had...met this officer in Kabul. He seemed a nice sort, a friend of the family. I realize now what an error in judgment I made."

"He is not under my command, I trust? I would have the knave drawn and quartered."

She detected sarcasm.

Kill him now!

"He...is not, and I should not wish to embarrass him."

"Admirable. Better and better, Miss Mozzhechkov. Or may I call you Katrina? And I am Pytyr."

And there it is, she realized. I can take this further. I can do so much if I play him along.

"Of course...Pytyr."

"Good," he said briskly, but his voice did not change. Katrina's skin would not stop crawling. "Where are you staying, in town, my dear? We would be glad to drop you off."

"I was staying with the man who left me stranded here, sir...Pytyr."

"I see. Then the only answer is for you to accompany my driver and me back to the garrison post until I can arrange accommodations for you in Parachinar first thing in the morning. Would that be satisfactory to a lady in distress?"

She forced herself to smile at the pig.

"Most satisfactory. I am no longer in distress, it would seem, thanks to you, Pytyr. I truly appreciate this."

"I'm sure you do. The corporal and I have but one, ah, bit of business to attend to, some people to meet. It won't take long. I beg your indulgence, and then we shall return to the fort and. . . but here we are. Corporal, do you recognize the turnoff beyond this tree?"

"Yes, sir," the driver replied.

The ZIL slowed and turned smoothly from the blacktop onto a rutted path. The limo continued off the highway.

The undulating terrain soon obscured the highway behind them, the headlights razoring a gash across stygian gloom, at last picking out a cluster of three men. They stood waiting for the ZIL in a loose half-circle across the path, holding rifles, not stepping aside when the limo approached.

The driver braked to a stop.

Katrina looked beyond him through the windshield, and thought her heart would hammer out of her chest when she recognized the *jukiabkr* from the village near Charikar where Tarik Khan's *mujahedeen* force had bivouacked the night before! The *jukiabkr* would recognize her and tell Voukelitch everything if he saw her.

At the moment he and the two Afghan hillmen with him could not see Katrina.

Then the driver snapped off the headlights.

It would take time for their eyes to readjust, Katrina realized. She held her shoulder bag close to her, her palm itching to feel the reassuring butt of the pistol within, but she had gambled this far and knew she would have to gamble some more or give up.

And she would never do that.

16

The driver killed the car engine.

A predawn breeze whistled softly through nearby pines.

"Do you wish me to get out with you, sir?" the corporal asked, not taking his eyes from the *mujahedeen* silhouetted in the starlight before him.

"Follow the plan," Voukelitch instructed his driver. "You know the signal?"

"Yes, sir."

"It begins, then." Voukelitch turned to Katrina and lifted her hand to kiss it gallantly. "Only a moment, my dear, I promise."

"Of course, Pytyr."

Voukelitch and Corporal Fet left the car.

Katrina remained in the tonneau. She casually lifted a hand to brush an errant strand of hair away from her forehead in the brief moment the interior light of the car went on.

Corporal Fet positioned himself close to the limo.

Voukelitch left the opposite side of the vehicle. He approached the waiting hillmen, who had not moved. His boots crunched the ground with his even strides, the only sound in the gloom.

The *jukiabkr* smelled as bad as ever to the Russian, a fetid combination of hashish and body odor.

The *jukiabkr* stepped forward.

His bodyguards remained behind, gripping their rifles in both hands, their eyes riveted unblinking on the general and the driver, who did not move from beside the car.

The *jukiabkr* kept a hand to his shoulder-strapped Kalashnikov rifle to facilitate swinging it around rapidly.

This hardly concerned Voukelitch. He read more greed than wariness in the faces of these men.

"You kept us waiting," the leader growled in his own tongue.

"We were delayed," the general replied in precise Pashto. I can use the bitch to advantage right now, he decided, and continued in the *jukiabkr*'s language. "A woman deserted on the highway. A very lovely woman."

The *jukiabkr* licked his lips.

"A . . . Russian woman?"

Voukelitch nodded.

"Very provocatively clothed. Would you like a glimpse, my friend? Or . . . more? She is my prisoner of sorts, though she does not know it yet, an enemy of the Soviet state. Perhaps I could share her with you."

The *jukiabkr* started toward the car.

"An excellent idea, my General. . . ."

Voukelitch lifted a hand to the man's arm, then quickly wiped his fingers on his uniform trousers.

"Ah, I would suggest business first though, my friend. And I understand you have arrived with information for me."

The Afghan turned reluctantly from the limousine to reach beneath the folds of his robe and produce a wrapped package. He extended the brick of hash to Voukelitch.

The Russian extended a wad of currency that quickly disappeared into the hillman's grasping hand, then into the voluminous robe.

The Afghan purred.

"A satisfactory transaction as always."

"And this information you have brought for me?" Voukelitch prodded.

The *jukiabkr* oiled a crafty smile.

"You will understand, surely, my General, that all things have a value."

Insolent swine, thought Voukelitch.

"And you will appreciate, friend *jukiabkr*, the value of trust. I shall determine the price of what you have to sell as in our other dealings. And above that, you can have the woman. I am done with her."

The hillman liked that.

Voukelitch had the desert snake right where he wanted him.

"I shall tell you then." The Afghan nodded, unable to keep his eyes from the dark windows of the limo.

The gray of false dawn etched the eastern hills in

sharp silhouette tinged with pink, not enough light for the *jukiabkr* to see the bait, and that made the lure all the more effective, Voukelitch knew.

"Be quick," he snapped. "I have a most busy day ahead of me. It is about the ambushed convoy last night, is it not? That happened near your village."

The *jukiabkr* forced his attention away from the car.

"You anticipate me. A force of *mujahedeen* led by Tarik Khan was responsible."

"Kabul must surmise as much," Voukelitch snapped again, impatient now for this to be over. As he spoke he angled toward the car. The *jukiabkr* accompanied him, the smuggler's bodyguards remaining at a suitable distance. "Tarik Khan is known to operate in the hills between Kabul and the Pass."

"An American traveled with Tarik Khan and his force, my General."

Voukelitch felt interest flicker in his eyes.

"What was his name?"

"One of my people heard him referred to as. . . Bolan. I have heard of this man, as have you, eh, General? Is this information not worth a handsome price?"

Voukelitch paused next to the rear door of the ZIL.

The Afghan did the same.

Voukelitch quelled a mixture of reactions, all of them indicating his immediate return to the base.

The Russian general had been willing to pass up

his visit to the brothel in Parachinar for what he would do to Katrina Mozzhechkov. He had considered not turning her in in exchange for certain favors. Then perhaps tomorrow, perhaps in a few days, he would contact Kabul after he grew bored with her.

Everything changed when he heard the name *Bolan*.

The general knew all about the Executioner's war against the KGB.

He could not accept that the Executioner's presence in Afghanistan, and the Devil's Rain project, which was about to begin, were unconnected.

It all made sense now: the man Lansdale, killed during a breakout staged, or so reports from Kabul claimed, by *one man*. This was not told to the rank and file, of course. But Voukelitch knew and had been too preoccupied with final preparations for tomorrow for it to register. But it registered now, and he knew he must make fast work of the *jukiabkr* and his men and the Mozzhechkov woman.

Security at the fort could not be left in the hands of the imbecile, Ghazi.

Bolan could already be in the area!

The KGB man paused for a moment with the *jukiabkr* beside the limo. He reached into a pocket and produced his cigarette holder and cigarettes as if idly fiddling while he considered. In fact, the lighting of the cigarette would be Corporal Fet's signal to open fire.

Voukelitch figured separating the leader from his bodyguards would be best. Katrina Mozzhechkov was the perfect bait, the only pity being that he would now have Fet kill her, too. Voukelitch had no time for dalliances, not with Mack Bolan in the area, and anyway, he reasoned, Kabul would be just as happy with a dead traitor as a live one.

He stepped nonchalantly away from the smuggler and reached for his lighter.

"Yes, I would say you have earned payment," he said, nodding as if reaching his decision, all the while easing back farther, pretending to make way for the *jukiabkr*'s access to the car. "I shall speak to my man about arranging payment. In the meantime—" Voukelitch motioned graciously to the car door "—amuse yourself with the woman. Do as you please. She is yours."

The *jukiabkr* smacked his lips noisier, sloppier than before.

"With pleasure, General."

He reached forward and opened the door.

The interior light went on to bathe Katrina Mozzhechkov in its spill. She was sitting with her back to the opposite door, facing the *jukiabkr*, one hand dipped into the purse she held against her like a shield.

Voukelitch raised his lighter but did not flick it. Not yet.

Corporal Fet leaned with his back against the front of the car in a casual pose, like a bored grunt waiting on his officer, but close to the open front window on the driver's side of the limo. Fet watched Voukelitch. He would not make his move until the lighter flared.

The general expected the *jukiabkr* to yank the woman from the limousine, then when Fet opened fire they would be done in at the same time as the bodyguards.

The Afghan hillman's eyes popped with surprise and his jaw dropped when he got a better look at the woman. He started to turn toward Voukelitch.

The *jukiabkr* began, ''She is the—''

Katrina drew the pistol from her purse and rapidly fired two shots.

The gunfire echoed hollowly inside the ZIL.

The bullets caught the hillman on the side of his head, pitching him to the ground; the surprised look stayed on his dead face.

Katrina scrambled from the far side of the ZIL.

The Afghan bodyguards, unable to tell from their position exactly what had happened, swung their rifles around as they dashed forward.

Voukelitch forgot about signals and the lighter and pawed for his side arm. He raced around the back of the car in an attempt to intercept the woman.

''Do it,'' the officer snarled at Fet. ''Now!''

Fet snaked a hand in through the car window and withdrew a Czech Model 23 submachine gun. He stepped away from the front of the car and planted himself squarely to open fire across the hood at the two hillmen.

The Afghans saw too late what Fet was up to, both starting to turn and track rifles in his direction with frantic pleas for him not to shoot.

He opened fire, the impact of so many bullets flinging the men off their feet into shrubbery nearby where only their legs protruded, tremulous in death.

General Voukelitch rounded the car with enough dispatch to intercept Katrina before she could bolt away from the vehicle. He closed in on her.

She turned and stood her ground, raising the pistol at him.

The officer rushed her before she could pull the trigger. He swatted the weapon from her hand with his own automatic.

Katrina's gun flew into the darkness. This time she turned, desperately trying to escape.

Voukelitch moved in before she could. He closed the distance, grabbed one of her wrists with his left hand and yanked her brutally so that she sprang back into him with an indignant, angry gasp. He wrenched her wrist hard around her body against the small of her back and painfully jerked her even more tightly against him.

She struggled to break free until he pressed the snout of his pistol's barrel against her temple. She felt it and stopped squirming.

Voukelitch glanced at Corporal Fet, who had

turned from massacring the Afghans. Fet held his fire when he saw the general had control of the situation.

The KGB man applied more pressure to emphasize his snarl close to Katrina's ear.

"The pig recognized you; that is why you shot him, is that not correct, my dear?"

"No! No! I hate these people. The way he looked at me—"

"Forget your deception," he raged, fighting back the urge to blow her head apart here and now, the treacherous bitch! "Katrina Mozzhechkov, enemy of the state. Yes, I know all about you, my pretty. You killed our friend the *jukiabkr* because he recognized you. You were with the man Bolan last night. And in Kabul?"

"Please, you are hurting me. . .it is all a mistake—"

Voukelitch's finger tensed around the trigger.

"It would be a mistake for you not to tell me what you know, Katrina. *I want Bolan.*"

Pytyr Voukelitch then felt the end of a pistol barrel pressed to his own temple.

"Surprise, comrade," growled a cold voice from hell. "You've got me."

17

The combined tracking skills of Bolan and Tarik Khan had traced the direction Katrina took from the last point any of the *mujahedeen* remembered having seen her, downhill toward the highway.

Her trail was easy enough for both men to read even in the dark that remained before the first hint of dawn to the east spread itself across the land.

Tarik Khan had at first been reluctant to follow the woman.

"My men can function here well on their own," he explained to Bolan, "but to my mind, the woman's disappearance but confirms what I have suspected from the beginning. She has never stopped being an agent for the Soviets. As for Mr. Lansdale: a ruse also. She knows you at least will follow and if you are isolated and killed, my people are back where we started with little chance of stopping the Devil's Rain in time without your assistance."

"I'm sorry, Tarik Khan," Bolan had replied respectfully, sincerely, "but I have to go with what I feel in my gut and in my heart as well as my head, as do you. And all three tell me Katrina is what she appears to be, a confused young woman who now has some idea of helping us on her own. But maybe all she'll do is blow our strategy to hell. She will definitely die if we don't get to her in time."

"But the mission— The attack on the garrison—"

"If I don't catch up with her in fifteen minutes, I'll return and we'll continue with the original plan. Set it back twenty-five minutes, that's all. I know time is short but we can afford this. I've got to afford it and I should be doing it instead of talking about it."

The guerrilla nodded.

"If you must, you should." He fell into step alongside the Executioner. They started out of the camp. "I have never known you to be wrong, *kuvii* Bolan. I know you from the field of battle and so I know you. Your intuition and compassion equal your bravery and skill. I will not let you go alone."

They had not gone far along the sloping terrain when they saw distant headlights leaving the Afghan army installation to turn in the direction of town.

When they saw the vehicle stop briefly, Bolan used his binoculars and at a distance of a half mile he witnessed the scene of Katrina intercepting the ZIL limo.

Katrina, you brave, irrational fool, thought Bolan.

He swallowed the lump of concern that constricted his throat and swung into action before the limo down there started rolling again.

"We've got to head off that car," he told Tarik Khan.

Both warriors hoped they would intercept the ZIL, considering the car's stop, some curves in the road that would slow its progress and the direct line taken by Tarik Khan and the Executioner who galloped to make good time across the rocky slope.

Bolan and Tarik Khan pulled up again when the limo, after traveling no more than a quarter mile, slowed for a turn off the highway to a point well in and concealed from the main road.

Bolan and the hillman had almost made it to the clearing where the ZIL had stopped when they heard the faint snap of muffled pistol shots followed by the louder sustained chatter of a submachine gun. The gunfire sounded to Bolan's trained ears like an Uzi or a Czech Model 23, and for a moment he feared he and Tarik Khan were too late. Then they made it over a rise and Bolan's NVD eyesight told him they had not arrived too late but not one damn microsecond too soon, either.

Bolan hand-signaled a maneuver.

Tarik Khan nodded his understanding and split off from the Executioner.

The two advanced undetected from different angles on an unfolding scene of action that Bolan took in at a glance: three dead Afghans, the Russian corporal at the front of the limo with the submachine gun and the Soviet officer grappling with Katrina, yanking her to him with his pistol to her

temple. The officer, a general no less, was so busy
struggling with the wildcat that he did not hear Bolan at all.

The Executioner pressed the muzzle of Big
Thunder to the guy's temple and everything
changed.

"Drop your weapon," Ice Voice growled. "Re-
lease the woman."

The Russian officer did both with alacrity, yet no
panic showed in the man's movements. Bolan knew
from this as much as from the photograph he had
seen of his target that this was the man he had come
to Afghanistan to kill.

The corporal, still clutching the SMG, did not
fire for fear of hitting his superior.

A shadow materialized behind the corporal.

Tarik Khan.

The corporal was completely oblivious of anyone
behind him until the Afghan hill fighter snaked his
left forearm around the man's neck. Tarik Khan
tilted the head forward into the crook of his arm,
then applied a fast open-handed punch behind the
man's ear.

The dry snap of the corporal's neck breaking
sounded like a pistol shot across the clearing. Tarik
Khan released the body and let it fall to the ground.
Then he turned to watch the others. Katrina was
standing a few feet away while Bolan kept the 11.5-
inch stainless steel cannon aimed in a straight-
armed stance at the Soviet officer's temple. The

Executioner was far enough away so the general could not try swinging around into Bolan or diving away from the gun.

With the bodyguard taken care of, Bolan stepped back from the officer, but the barrel of Big Thunder never wavered from the Russian's head.

"Turn around, comrade," Bolan ordered. "General Voukelitch, I presume."

The officer turned with deliberate movement to acknowledge Bolan with a nod.

"The infamous Executioner," Voukelitch returned with cool formality. "You have a habit, it would seem, of appearing when and where you are least expected."

Bolan glanced at Tarik Khan, who reached down almost absently to relieve the dead corporal of his SMG and ammo clips before moving to the car, where an Afghan lay sprawled in death.

"We are a good team, you and I," the *mujahedeen* leader gruffed. He used one foot to flop the corpse over onto its back so he could get a look at the dead face. "We knew this one, *kuvii* Bolan. Allah has a sense of justice, you see. It is your friend of the hash breath."

Bolan glanced at Katrina.

"Are you okay?"

She nodded, found her H&K automatic where it had fallen and retrieved it.

"The *jukiabkr* is an informer and a smuggler of drugs. They were going to...." Her voice faltered at what had almost happened. She looked to Bolan for understanding. "I wanted to. . . ."

"The thing that matters now is that you have proved yourself to *malik* Tarik Khan," Bolan interrupted kindly.

He glanced at the hill chief who sauntered over.

Tarik Khan grunted with a last look at the dead *jukiabkr*.

"She has proved herself," he agreed.

General Voukelitch cleared his throat.

"Pardon my impertinence, gentlemen, but may I inquire what is to become of me? Am I to be murdered like my driver?"

"Not if you cooperate," Bolan white-lied to the cannibal. "There's a reason I suggested my friend use his hands to kill the corporal. You're my ticket onto that fort, comrade. Cover him, Tarik Khan. If he so much as twitches an eye wrong, kill him. We can find another way onto the base."

Tarik Khan centered his rifle on the general's heart.

"It will be difficult to restrain myself."

"Do your best." Bolan walked over to the sprawled corpse of the driver. "Looks like a close enough fit to pass."

Voukelitch raised his hands to assure Tarik Khan that he meant to cooperate. The officer retained the expression of a stone wall but his apprehension under Tarik Khan's close-up loathing said he almost preferred the cool-eyed aim behind the AutoMag.

Bolan hurriedly shed his combat webbing and lightweight munitions and equipment and shucked them through the open driver's window onto the floor of the ZIL, along with his silenced MAC-10.

He made quick work of stripping the trousers and tunic from the dead soldier. He slipped them over his blacksuit. He had instructed Tarik Khan with hand signals to slay the soldier without a weapon so as not to get any blood on the uniform.

Voukelitch watched Bolan.

When the Executioner returned to the group the general risked a snicker as Bolan pulled off his NVD goggles and slid them into a pocket of the blacksuit before buttoning up the tunic.

"You hope to bluff your way onto the installation?"

"With your help, General. Maybe not if it was a Soviet base, but I saw this vehicle slide out of there a while ago without even stopping for the guards at the gate. The militia sentries saw you coming and had the gate open to salute you through as nice as you please. That's the way they'll do it on your way back in."

Voukelitch lowered his upraised hands. Steel prodded his spine.

"I am a Soviet officer. I will not betray—"

Katrina interrupted.

"He deals in hashish," she said, glaring in accusation. "He has a brick of it on his person. He paid the hillman for it. These pigs barter in all manner of death; violent, and the kind that rots a civilization from within."

"We'll let the general keep his hash," Bolan decided. He unholstered Big Thunder again and the .44's muzzle retracked to the cannibal. "If he dies today, it will give them a little more to cover up and reorganize and panic about and I like that."

Tarik Khan glanced at his wristwatch.

"Has anything...changed?" he asked Bolan, careful not to divulge reference to the scheduled assault.

"Nothing, except spare the choppers at the landing pad. They're mine."

The hillman's brow furrowed but he nodded.

"As you say, my brother. And the woman?"

"Take her with you." Bolan glanced at Katrina. "You must go with him."

She nodded without hesitation.

"I will. A soul has been redeemed here...and I am wiser for it."

"No more talk. Good luck, both of you. You had best return," he advised Tarik Khan.

"And so we shall."

The Afghan fighter stalked off.

Katrina looked as if she wanted to say something to the nightfighter who had saved her life but she knew Bolan was right. She followed Tarik Khan into the gloom.

Bolan glanced at the ridge of metallic gray inching higher behind the eastern peaks.

Fifteen minutes until the first half-light of dawn started to nibble at the dark, he gauged.

He gestured with the AutoMag to the KGB man.

"In the car, General. In the back like a nice passenger, and no sudden moves."

Voukelitch walked to the car. He stood aside while Bolan covered him and made a fast, thorough search of the tonneau for any hidden weapon or signaling device.

Bolan stood back and motioned Voukelitch inside.

The Russian general got in without a word.

Bolan hurried to get in behind the steering wheel. He twisted the rearview mirror so he had a full-length view of the shadowy form of his passenger.

Bolan started the limo, backed it around and drove toward the highway. He holstered the AutoMag, reached to his shoulder holster, now concealed beneath the Soviet uniform, and drew the silenced Beretta 93-R. He hefted the Beretta for emphasis where Voukelitch could see it.

"Here's how it is, General. We roll onto the base and you take me to the Devil's Rain. Keep your mouth shut and do as you're told, do you read me?"

He lowered the Beretta to the seat beside him, his finger on the trigger while he drove with his other hand.

Voukelitch reached with extreme nonchalance for a pocket of his uniform jacket.

"May I smoke?"

"You may not." Ice Voice stopped him. Bolan steered onto the highway in the direction of the fort a mile and a half away. "The Devil's Rain. Where is it on the base?"

"And why should I tell you?"

"You may not have to. You'll have it in or adjacent to the HQ where you keep an eye on things and still play the bigshot with your own office, if you run to type, General."

"It seems I do," bristled Voukelitch, his voice getting more confident the closer they got to the lights of the fort. "Not that the information will do you much good. Even the fabled Executioner will not penetrate the security with which I have surrounded the lab. You are already a dead man, Mack Bolan."

"And so are you," Bolan grunted.

He took his eyes from the road ahead to glance over his shoulder. The Beretta 93-R tracked around on the cannibal in the back seat. Voukelitch started to cry out, suddenly realizing the mortal mistake he had made in admitting that Bolan had been right about the location of the lab.

The silenced Beretta coughed discreetly.

The savage ceased all motion except to relax back into the upholstered corner of the tonneau, remaining in an upright position, the head dropped forward, chin touching the chest as if the general were catching a short nap and not the big sleep.

Bolan returned his attention to his driving.

He holstered the Beretta and drove on toward the floodlit fort.

18

Bolan steered General Voukelitch's ZIL limo through the front gates, onto the Afghan militia base. The sleepy-eyed militia regulars extended the same courtesy to the officer's car going in as they had when Bolan had watched the car leave the fort earlier.

Apparently the general's zipping out and into town at odd hours was not unusual.

Bolan slowed to a moderate speed, hoping like hell the corpse of the KGB gangster would not choose this precise moment to tip over and draw suspicion from the guardhouse.

But as Bolan drove through he doubted if even that would have aroused any interest from the dullards at the front gate. Any other vehicle would no doubt have received its share of hassle but not the general's wagon coming home at this morning hour. Bolan spotted three sentries, two of them not even rousting themselves from the guard shack to come out; one of the two looked asleep.

Some army the Kabul regime has raised, thought Bolan. Though with the walls and heavy machine guns in those towers and with parapets along the walls set up for more firepower, he read the fort as secure enough from any full-scale standard assault from the outside.

He steered the limo to a stop in front of a two-story plain brick building that had to be base headquarters, judging from the insignias and flag painted above the door, poor cousin to the Soviet base in Kabul. A new-looking one-level prefab structure stood adjacent to the building.

The lab.

The Devil's Rain.

The landing pad in front of HQ still hosted the two Soviet choppers, dark and deserted, and beyond them Bolan saw the two-story barracks building that stretched the width of the far side of the base.

No lights shone in the barracks building yet, but that would change any second.

The other structures on the base were dark except for headquarters and the adjacent laboratory.

Bolan turned off the limo's lights and ignition. He grabbed the combat webbing and MAC-10 and started to open his car door to get out when a man emerged from the front entrance to the HQ.

A militia officer, a major, obviously waiting for General Voukelitch's return, strode briskly to the rear door on the passenger side of the limo.

The Afghan major opened the door, leaned in and started to speak to a man he did not know was dead.

"General, I must say I had hoped you would forgo your. . .proclivities at such an auspicious moment," the Afghan began in a tone of respectful peevishness, then he noted the bullet hole in Voukelitch's uniform over the heart. The Afghan blinked and turned to Bolan. "What—" he began.

Bolan reached back to clamp iron-hard fingers around the major's throat; the man wore a security clearance badge, no doubt the Devil's Rain project, identifying him as Major Ghazi, Base Commandant.

The Executioner applied pressure and tugged the man into the limo with practically no noise at all except for Ghazi's wheeze as he tried frantically, futilely to grab at Bolan's choking hands; then this cannibal, Afghan variety, died before he could do even that.

Ghazi's corpse sprawled across Voukelitch's lap.

Bolan closed the passenger door after Ghazi and left the two cannibals as they were.

He debarked from the ZIL, the webbing of munitions packets slung over his left shoulder, the Ingram MAC-10 hugged in close to his right side, but in a manner that would not present a suspicious figure to anyone watching as "the general's driver" left the ZIL to allow Major Ghazi and General Voukelitch to confer.

The veil of darkness had yielded to the first strange half-light of day. The chatter of night insects turned into birdcalls chirping beyond the fortress walls.

"Corporal" Bolan stalked businesslike, all correct military bearing as befitted the driver of a KGB general, toward the prefab structure.

No one appeared to intercept him.

He doubted if anyone paid attention to him except for a militia regular, a kid of no more than fifteen, who was standing sentry duty.

Bolan knew there would be plenty heavy security beyond this outside door. This kid had been placed here so as not to draw undue suspicion to where the Devil's Rain was brewed.

The sentry looked like forced draftee material. He eyeballed the uniform of the approaching driver and did not even bother to unshoulder his AK-47 when he started to ask the "corporal" something.

The kid realized something was wrong too late.

Bolan did not slow his stride past the sentry. He brought his right fist up in a swift blow that caught the soldier on the chin, snapped his head back with a thunk into a wall, and the kid's eyes rolled back until only the whites showed.

The Executioner spared lives when he could, like now, even from the opposing side. If Bolan read this kid's history right, this recruit was as much a victim of the Soviets as the civilians Bolan's blitz was meant to help, and if Bolan was wrong that was the kid's problem.

The Man from Blood pushed the sagging, unconscious guard around the side of the building, out of sight of anyone passing by. The sentry would not go unnoticed for long, but Bolan had no intention of staying around for long, either.

He hit the locked door of the lab with a kick that sent the panel ripping inward off its hinges, grabbing the immediate attention of three Soviet infantrymen who stood guard in the short hallway. Beyond a glass-partitioned door Bolan saw activity; men in white moving about.

He concentrated on the real security of General Voukelitch's hellspawn: three *raydoviki* who had not been lounging but still were caught off guard by the sudden Bolan assault.

Two of them tracked rifles toward the blitzer with blinding speed.

The third reached frantically for a red button near a wall phone that had to be connected to an alarm.

Bolan shot off the soldier's arm with a burst from the silenced Ingram, severing it at the shoulder when the index finger was an inch away from the button. The uniform-sleeved meat plopped to the floor, extended index finger pointing spasmodically, a fountain of murky gore spurting from the ragged stump at the shoulder.

The man's expression expanded with shock when he saw the arm, then the expression exploded under a hail of .45-caliber shredders that continued to cut down the other two before either could trigger a shot. The three dead men tangoed in death throes before they collapsed, spreading slimy pools of blood that Bolan sidestepped.

He powerhoused another kick with enough rage to splinter the inside door to the lab. He stormed in with flame snarling from the MAC suppressor, the Ingram chugging flesh-eaters at a rate of 1,145 rounds per minute as Bolan scoped the scene and picked targets.

A laboratory, yeah. White-smocked, bespectacled egghead types were working around a five-foot-high aluminum tub—Bolan estimated the diameter at fifteen feet—filled to six inches from the brim with a stinking greenish-black liquid that could only be what Bolan had traveled all this way to destroy.

The Devil's Rain.

He counted five cannibals working a console of gauges and lights that controlled the flow of the junk through pipes and a processing system to a dock where a half dozen Afghan army regulars trundled oblong canisters that looked like bombs onto wheeled flatcars, which would be used to get the stuff to the choppers.

Bolan took out the soldiers first, deciding not to spare any of these punks. They would be the ones to fire on the blitzer if they could reach their rifles, which were stacked while they worked under the watchful eye of two more *raydoviki*.

The two Russians caught the blitzer's death-hail first, then the Ingram tracked on to eat away at the other soldiers who withered under the .45-caliber bullets in various stages of reaction before any of them could fire a shot.

Bolan slammed a fresh 30-round magazine into the Ingram and a new fury gripped him. He tracked on the killers of women, children and the elderly that the slave state could not enslave and wanted dead; animals who thought they were far enough away from the death, suffering and other abominations they cursed mankind with; horrors like the Devil's Rain and Yellow Rain.

But Bolan dirtied these scum plenty, .45-caliber steel bursting white smocks apart in exploding red fountains, cannibals toppling in all directions like bowling pins after a strike.

Bolan punched another magazine in and tracked up at the last man in white who stood at a gauge panel on the walkway ten feet above the black-green shit in the tub.

This one had hidden himself from Bolan's line of view and punched a button up there that started an ululating siren piercing outside somewhere. Then the savage got brave when he thought he had the drop on Bolan and pegged off a round from a pistol. The bullet cracked too close to Bolan.

At the last second before Bolan demolished that face, the Executioner pedigreed the guy.

Dr. Gregor Golodkin.

The Soviet's leading specialist in chemical weapons and their use, most lately in Afghanistan.

There is only one way for this cannibal to go.

Bolan lowered his aim and triggered a sideways burst before the baby killer could fire again. Golodkin's legs flailed out from under him. A scream that started from the bad doctor's panicky mouth erupted with new intensity in the eye blink he had to realize he was falling over the railing into the tub of Devil's Rain. The bloodcurdling yell was interrupted by the splash as he went under, and all that came up was a bubbling, dissolving thing that sizzled like frying bacon. The human mess melted into nothing and a foul cloud rose to mark the passing.

Bolan placed a wad of plastic explosive at the base of the tank and timed it.

The wailing of the siren from outside needled him to the dock where the canisters stood. The containers would be pressurized; they would go with the blow from the explosives.

He raced past the canisters and dived from the dock. He had set the explosives by the tank for ten seconds.

His last impression before the explosion was confused shouting as soldiers poured in from the entrance in response to the siren.

The blast hurled Bolan into the air and he felt carried along on a hot wind. The earth shook and everything related to the Devil's Rain blew into a maelstrom of sense-reeling destruction that engulfed the soldiers and the lab.

The Executioner landed in a well-practiced somersault, riding the momentum of his leap and the force of the blast, coming out of it into a beeline run around the far corner of the lab building. He had drawn on what he knew about the shit they were brewing back there to set his explosives in such a way that the building would not be destroyed. Contamination from the Devil's Rain seemed to require bodily contact, not inhalation; none of the hellspawners in the lab had been wearing gas masks.

The initial response to the explosion would be for them to work like hell to contain the liquid horror to the lab building, a diversion Bolan hoped would help him.

He continued away from the lab across the rear length of the headquarters building. He came around the front of the far end of the HQ from where army soldiers poured toward the lab exactly as Bolan had hoped. He wasted no time. He cut off on another direct course full speed toward the nearer of the two helicopters.

The eerie visibility of the new dawn etched a surreal sharpness to the shriek of an incoming missile as one of the gun houses exploded into flying mortar, gun parts and airborne bodies everywhere.

The echoes of the explosion yielded to heavy machine-gun fire, and more incoming rockets from Tarik Khan's *mujahedeen* punched at the walls and other watchtowers but not at the landing pad and the gunships, as Bolan had requested.

Confusion reigned across the fort.

On his dash toward the choppers Bolan saw that the bodies of Voukelitch and the camp commandant had been discovered in the ZIL cannibal car.

That left a big hole in response coordination, some troopers charging to the parapets to defend the fort, others fanning out around the lab, everyone disorganized and confused.

The only resistance Bolan met was from four Soviet crewmen who had been waiting near the choppers, ready to spread death and then fly safely away. They looked as confused as everyone else at the sudden attack, but their reaction time flared fast when they spotted the Executioner jogging toward them. But the approaching figure wore a Soviet uniform and so these death merchants held their fire and Bolan exterminated the lice safely into hell.

He tossed a grenade from the cluster of munitions webbing into the hatchway of the chopper several hundred feet away. He scored a bull's-eye, the grenade demolishing the interior of that craft, lifting it off its landing rails, the machine settling back down where it would stay disabled.

Bolan leaped through the side hatch door of the other chopper. He rushed to the cockpit. He had a working knowledge of helicopters dating back to the war in Nam.

He got the attention of most every soldier inside the fort when he gunned the big bird to life, filling the cacophony of battle with a rotor throb that grew louder when he skipped the warm-up phase. He felt the chopper wobble about him more than it should, but the bird lifted and Bolan hoped Tarik

Khan's force had sense enough to see Bolan pirating the helicopter.

They did. The incoming missile fire wrought havoc all around but did not strike the chopper as it gained an altitude of several hundred feet.

Bullets punctured the chopper as Bolan banked it around, but most of the firepower down there was still directed at the hills, the parapets filled with soldiers despite the steady toppling of men from incoming fire. Most of the Afghan soldiers Bolan saw beyond the chopper's Plexiglas probably thought the chopper was piloted by one of their own to give them air cover.

No such luck.

Bolan banked the death bird around in a low sweep, triggering missiles and rockets that streaked from the gunship at anything in his sights. The intensified holocaust gnawed at man and brick down there like a mountain lion chomping a field mouse, decimating the garrison and the fort into slaughter and pandemonium in less than two minutes of unleashed wrath.

The incoming mortar, rocket and heavy machine-gun fire continued without letup.

Bolan worked the controls to bank the copter away from the fort haloed in black smoke from fires that pillared into the sky.

Bolan piloted the bird on a wide swing around Tarik Khan's force along the ridge overlooking the besieged fort. He set the chopper down at a safe distance behind the staggered line of well-hidden *mujahedeen* who kept hammering nonstop at the fort.

Katrina Mozzhechkov and Tarik Khan hurried to the chopper from where they had watched it land.

An occasional explosion geysered earth as return fire from the fort impacted the ground around the *mujahedeen*'s position. But firepower from the garrison had slacked off considerably since there were not that many men and artillery remaining down there.

The woman and the leader of the hill fighters crouched under the idling rotors and joined Bolan in the chopper.

"Your men have good aim," Bolan shouted to Tarik Khan over the engine noise. "This machine will get us the short hop to the border."

"The Devil's Rain?"

"Destroyed. Voukelitch had his security tight on this. He had to be sitting on everything connected to the operation. The Devil's Rain and those who spawned it are no more."

"It is good," the hillman intoned. "But there is no time. Soviet fighter jets are scrambling for here as we speak. My force can disperse to nearby caves, but you must be gone." The resistance fighter placed a hand on Bolan's shoulder; one fraternal squeeze that spoke everything. "Until we meet again, Executioner." Then he looked at Katrina. "And my thanks to you, woman. I have learned from you. Goodbye."

Tarik Khan left the chopper and stalked away without looking back.

Bolan revved up the engines again. He glanced at Katrina.

"Hang on, lady. Get set for a rough ride."

She grabbed a seat and a wall strap next to him. Bolan saw her direct a steady gaze across the scene of battle and it told him this special woman had confronted and defeated her demons. All that was left for her now was the future.

"I'm ready," she assured him. "For anything."

The engine rumbled and the copter lifted off.

Bolan gave Tarik Khan a last salute from on high that the resistance fighter returned, then the hillman turned to join his men and Bolan control-sticked them up and away from there.

He piloted the chopper at full throttle across the blue sky of a new day, skimming the jagged, treacherous terrain low enough to avoid Soviet radar.

Toward the border frontier.

Toward Pakistan.

Mission completed, yeah.

And toward the mourning of too many lost in the name of freedom that fired a strange, savage, noble people to resist impossible odds.

Lansdale.

Alja Malikyar.

So many more.

They had not died in vain.

Their sacrifice kept the flame alive and it would

burn longer and more brightly now without Devil's Rain to douse it.

Yeah, Tarik Khan, thought Executioner Bolan. Until next time.

Excerpts from
THE PENDLETON TAPES

The first of an occasional series

We, the publishers of the Executioner books, are not prepared to let posterity alone chronicle the insights into the thinking of Don Pendleton, creator of Mack Bolan. Why should literature become valuable only with the passage of time? Why should we have to wait to pay tribute to something that we enjoy so much in the here and now?

At Gold Eagle, we know the moral value of what Don Pendleton is saying through the character of Mack Bolan. And we know that the message conveyed by his work will endure through time.

Any believer in our basic freedoms will recognize the efforts of Mack Bolan to preserve and protect those very freedoms that we cherish. Here, then, is a self-portrait of the artist. Listen to him.

I have a habit of talking aloud at a period of development in a book when I've written myself into a corner from which there's no logical escape. Then I'll sit down and turn on a tape recorder and just simply unreel my own mind, and in this talking-out process I find my way out of the problem. That is the origin of these tapes, and is the source of the thoughts recorded in them.

I am very much aware that in the general readership of the Executioner books there does exist a number of young people. Some of the readers are even fifth, sixth graders. Of course I cannot and will not direct my writing at the level of the fifth grader; these books are aimed at the adult mind. But personally I don't see anything wrong with young people reading these books. My own kids read the books.

I use the four-letter words that seem to be expected of my characters. It should be noted that Mack Bolan does not use profanity except in those instances where he's pretending to be one of the enemy. Some of the kids who have been reading the books have pointed out to me the difference in Bolan as Bolan compared with Bolan as a Mafioso. Kids pick up on such things, and there is a very definite moral in that particular facet of the books.

I keep my hero clean. I give him the higher human attributes, and I depict his war as a motivated crusade with decidedly human overtones. I show this man in almost continuous conflict with himself. I am not exhorting anyone to emulate Mack Bolan. He lives a grim life. The character is built around one basic idea: that here is a man who has submerged his own life into his mission. He has sacrificed everything that he holds dear. He's a man who has forgone everything, all his dreams, everything, to fling himself into his war.

THE HUMAN RACE has not come that far that we can all live in complete harmony with one another. There are going to be differences between people. There are going to be people who will resort to violence to get their own way. This is the situation in the Executioner books.

Bolan did not suddenly decide to go out and start shooting people. His crusade is a reaction to violence of a very destructive nature. He looks upon his war as a constructive war.

I'm a peaceful man. I don't go around knocking heads, but I do recognize there are limits beyond which I will not remain a peaceful man. If someone breaks into my house with an ax in his hand, bent on hacking up my family and myself and I happen to have a .45 nearby that

I can get to, I'm going to kill that dude before he can cut my family down. I trust that this approach would be shared by most people.

There is always a line beyond which any human being cannot be pushed and still keep his ideals intact. This is one of Bolan's continual conflicts. He is a man of high ideals. He does have a reverence for life and that is why he's at war. He believes that it's the wrong people who are violent in our society—the hoods and the crooks, not the protectors of society.

Something very important is taking place here on this obscure little planet. Life has tremendous meaning. I believe that the good life is the challenged life, not the easy one. I think that in their deeper values my Executioner books reflect this philosophy. I have tried to use highly dramatic situations to bring out the deeper values that are inherent in all human life.

In that sense the Executioner books are a testament to the human spirit. I sweat and agonize over my phrases as much as any writer who ever lived. I change, rewrite, revise, carry on as though I were writing the great American novel. I work very conscientiously with great pains to put together prose that has no ambiguity in its meaning. My team is producing hard-hitting, edge-of-the-seat, eyeball-jerking fiction. It's not the guys who write "by the book" who write the books that sell, that are meaningful. It's the guys who say to hell with what I'm supposed to do who are doing it the way it should be done. I intend to maintain that spirit in these books for as long as Mack Bolan may live. And I think my readers, from the very youngest to the oldest, would expect no less of me.

HE'S EXPLOSIVE.
HE'S MACK BOLAN...

He learned his deadly skills in Vietnam...then put them to good use by destroying the Mafia in a blazing one-man war. Now **Mack Bolan** ventures further into the cold to take on his deadliest challenge yet—the KGB's worldwide terror machine.

Follow the lone warrior on his exciting new missions... and get ready for more nonstop action from his high-powered combat teams: **Able Team**—Bolan's famous Death Squad—battling urban savagery too brutal and volatile for regular law enforcement. And **Phoenix Force**—five extraordinary warriors handpicked by Bolan to fight the dirtiest of antiterrorist wars, blazing into even greater danger.

Fight alongside these three courageous forces for freedom in all-new action-packed novels! Travel to the gloomy depths of the cold Atlantic, the scorching sands of the Sahara, and the desolate Russian plains. You'll feel the pressure and excitement building page after page, with nonstop action that keeps you enthralled until the explosive conclusion!

Now you can have all the new Gold Eagle novels delivered right to your home!

You won't want to miss a single one of these exciting new action-adventures. And you don't have to! Just fill out and mail the card at right and we'll enter your name in the Gold Eagle home subscription plan. You'll then receive six brand-new action-packed Gold Eagle books every other month, delivered right to your home! You'll get two Mack Bolan novels, one Able Team and one Phoenix Force, plus one book each from two thrilling, new Gold Eagle libraries, **SOBs** and **Track**. In **SOBs** you'll meet the legendary team of mercenary warriors who fight for justice and win. **Track** is a rugged, compassionate, highly-skilled adventurer. He's a good man in a bad world, a world in which desperate affairs require desperate remedies, and he's got just the prescription.

FREE! The New War Book and Mack Bolan bumper sticker.
FREE AUTOMAG the Magazine of Action-Adventure. This informative newsletter is filled with previews of upcoming books, inside news about your favorite Gold Eagle characters and much, much more about the world of action-adventure.

As soon as we receive your card we'll rush you the long-awaited New War Book and Mack Bolan bumper sticker—both ABSOLUTELY FREE. Then under separate cover, you'll receive your six Gold Eagle novels and your copy of Automag.

The New War Book is *packed* with exciting information for Bolan fans: a revealing look at the hero's life...two new short stories...book character biographies...even a combat catalog describing weapons used in the novels! The New War Book is a special collector's item you'll want to read again and again. And it's yours FREE when you mail your card!

Of course, you're under no obligation to buy anything. Your first six books come on a 10-day free trial—if you're not thrilled with them, just return them and owe nothing. The New War Book, and Automag and bumper sticker are yours to keep, FREE!

Don't miss a single one of these thrilling novels...mail the card now, while you're thinking about it.

HE'S UNSTOPPABLE. AND HE'LL FIGHT AGAINST ALL ODDS TO DEFEND FREEDOM!

Mail this coupon today!